RESTLESS
SPURS

by

ARCHIE JOSCELYN

The War Between the States was at an end, and Mike McChesney was not the only man to find out, after surviving the rigors of battle, that the future held little assurance of glory or even of tranquillity. But because he had been a soldier, he continued to serve, although demoted in rank, and to wage his own personal war against those fellow officers who shared neither his Irish dreams nor his trust in the average man, be he Indian or white.

RESTLESS SPURS

RESTLESS SPURS

by

ARCHIE JOSCELYN

PRESTIGE BOOKS
NEW YORK, NEW YORK

FOR PAM

Prestige Books, Inc.
18 East 41st Street, New York, New York 10017

Printed in the United States of America

RESTLESS SPURS

1.

This was the time when the streams ran softly, the Moon of the Changing Season, with the long cold of winter lying just over the horizon. It came to Mike McChesney, lean, tall and easy in the saddle, that he was beginning to think like an Indian; in some respects to see and feel as they would. In that he found nothing bad, nothing of which to be ashamed, although Major Orlando Overton, riding half a length ahead, might well regard him askance for holding such views.

Ordinarily this was the time of year which he liked best, the season when the long, hot days of summer merged into fall, into nights of a thousand dreams. The creeks which had drunk too deeply, turning riotous, were now placidly introspective, poking wet fingers among tree roots, rippling the water grasses, caressing moss-bearded stones as they passed. He had the fancy that the wildly hurrying waters of spring had sent back word that the sea would wait, that after all, it was not so great a heaven; better to loiter where there was so much to see and enjoy along the way; life and events which, once past, might never be reclaimed.

Perhaps it was the Irish in him, a poetic turn of mind which years of war and discipline had subdued but never quite submerged. Riding with the major, with a part of East Company and a portion of Charley trotting behind, half his mind loped ahead like a hunting coyote; the other half hesitated and swung back, questing amid memory's thickets for morsels overlooked or only half devoured.

He was Lieutenant McChesney, and that dream was as faded as the uniform he wore. Not too many years before he had been Major McChesney, breveted a colonel; sometimes, when the stress of war was not too great, dreaming—that Irish heritage again— of still greater things, such as the shimmering height of general command.

Since then he had learned, only too well, the old, old lesson. The paths of glory—rutted, rocky trails at best—led not up, but down.

Many another officer, at war's end, had accepted demotion as the alternative to leaving the service. George Armstrong Custer, now a lieutenant-colonel, had been a brigadier. Major Overton had been a colonel, breveted a general. Accordingly, his probable awareness that Mike McChesney had served at a higher rank had not impressed him.

McChesney sensed unplumbed depths in Overton. Heavily handsome, the stubbornness of a full-fleshed chin was belied by the indecision of the mouth above.

He could be charming—but so, on occasion, could a rattlesnake. McChesney was coming to know him, on this overlong scout, but he was still far from understanding the man.

The land lay wide, a long expanse of plain and plateau, symbolic of God's mercy, having neither beginning nor end. Such fancies, McChesney had long since learned to keep to himself. Few who knew him guessed at the man beneath the surface. Most respected him for his competence and a wide and varied knowledge ranging well beyond the purely military. Major Overton had all but confessed as much when welcoming him to Fort Lookout a few weeks before. Designated Outlook, the name had been inverted as more grimly appropriate to the place.

In need of another officer, Overton had requested the transfer of McChesney to his command, both because of his record and his familiarity with Indians and their customs.

That had appeared to form a sound basis for a good working relationship between them. But already McChesney had his doubts. Intuitively he suspected that similar doubts might be coursing the bloodstream which fed the major's brain.

By contrast with his dark-haired lieutenant, whose face, smooth-shaven save for a sandy mustache, lent an illusion of youthfulness belied by the record, Orlando Overton was almost flambuoyant, with long

red hair falling almost to his shoulders, eyes as blue
as the skies of autumn peering from under craggy
thickets; a flashing smile which could be followed
by a whip-sharp reprimand. Overton's big horse,
though wordless, told its own story. Its sides were
scarred by the teeth of spurs, even as those prongs
held the rustiness of dried blood.

As he stared ahead to a horizon misleadingly empty in appearance, the tangle of sun was in Overton's
eyes, its glitter as probing as the points of his ever-
restless spurs. He suspected that his lieutenant had
put away dreams and once-cherished ambitions as
a man puts away childish hopes. Which was well
enough for ordinary mortals. As for himself setbacks
served only to sharpen his ambition. He rode today
with a strong hope and a growing certainty that before this sweep was ended he'd be on his way again,
on the climb to promotion.

That might take some doing, but with opportunity
at hand, he would not hesitate to grasp it. A thistle
lost its sting only when seized ruthlessly.

His glance swiveled to the dust-stained troopers
riding behind, pausing on Sergeant Seamus O'Reilly,
at the moment a horse's length behind McChesney,
his gaze fixed on the unconscious back of the lieutenant. Unaware that he was watched in turn, the
bitter black eyes of the sergeant blazed with hate,
naked and virulent. Because Seamus O'Reilly was
first of all a soldier, and Mike McChesney was also

a soldier and his superior, O'Reilly would not make the most of whatever opportunity might be offered to slip a length of steel in McChesney's back or between his ribs. But that was not to say that he would not enjoy doing so.

O'Reilly had a seemingly careless gift of words. He'd questioned him aimlessly, then eagerly, as between fellow-Irishmen, then more probingly, his initial liking giving way to contempt, disillusion to brooding, bitter rancor. He felt it now like the sharp pang of heartburn and shifted his gaze to the emptiness of the distant horizon.

To some men there were grays and browns, degrees of good or evil, but to Seamus O'Reilly there were black and whites and nothing between. A man named Mike McChesney should be fully Irish, imbued with hatred for the English across a thousand bitter years, a wearer of the green, an adherent to the Holy Church. Those were the marks of a son of the Old Sod.

But McChesney had confessed innocently, even naively, that his father had been Ulster-born and reared, and Protestant; he had all but granted that he might discern beauty in the bright hue of orange. Renegade and heretic he accordingly was, even though Father Flanagan had once childed O'Reilly for having such un-Christian thoughts. One made allowance for the cloth of the clergy. An Orangeman was a traitor, and traitors were to be killed. And some day, perhaps—

McChesney had grown aware of the sergeant's dislike and the reasons for it. He had shrugged them off lightly—perhaps too carelessly. After all, they were soldiers, and rank and discipline prevailed, as was necessary.

O'Reilly's glance shifted to the broad back of the major. The glare faded from his eyes and was replaced by a covert admiration. Overton too was a Protestant, but since he was not Irish, in him such error was excusable. On other matters, O'Reilly had long since discovered, their views had a way of jibing.

Ostensibly they were riding on a tour of inspection, making a wide sweep of the land, to observe and to be seen; not quite a scout, nor precisely an expedition, but something of both. They aimed to impress the restless redskins, reminding them that chastisement could come swiftly, that retribution for wrongdoing was as certain as the winter which lurked in the offing, growing nearer with each passing day.

Seamus O'Reilly was Catholic in more than religion; he hated on an all but universal scale, though reserving his bitterest animosity for "niggers" and "diggers." It was true that he had fought through the war in a blue uniform, and one result had been to free the blacks. But he'd taken no pleasure in that fact, shrugging the thing aside as a political necessity of the moment; a misjudgment on the part of man whom in essence he despised.

Digger Indians were the poorest specimens of humanity—if one misguidedly designated them as human—whom he had ever encountered—filthy, poverty-stricken, barely existing. That such unfortunates might prove to be generous and kindly had failed to impress him. With them, sweepingly, he classed all tribes and peoples whose skin was stained with color.

His smoldering eyes lightened. Like other beasts of the field, they were good for one thing: sport. He anticipated sweeping over and among them, plying sword, discharging his pistol. Unless he was badly mistaken, there'd be some killing of Indians before this sweep was finished.

For the moment, prudence dictated that they ride simply and merely as a scouting party. The hastily put-together portions of two companies were hardly fit for anything beyond a possible skirmish. The land looked empty, but O'Reilly had long since learned how deceptive appearances could be. Plenty of Indians were abroad, from many tribes— Cheyenne, Arapaho, Piegan, Crow, Blackfeet, Sioux—those and others. They were as restless as birds when the winds of migration blew, as hungry as beasts about to hibernate and, like them, apprehensive of the long cold. They strayed from reservations as though such invisible boundary lines did not exist.

And they might as well not exist, McChesney reflected, the same thread of thought running through his own mind. White men, with few exceptions, respected the sanctuary of such lines only when it suited their purpose. Otherwise they ignored them and trespassed, so it was hardly logical to expect the Indians to show more concern on their part—particularly when their promised rations were scant or not forthcoming, when starvation was not merely a possibility but a dire threat.

At such times they sought their old hunting grounds, hopeful of securing meat as a provision against the long winter. Meat was becoming more and more scarce, as hide or tongue hunters slaughtered the bison by the tens of thousands, leaving the carcasses to rot, a stench in the nostrils of all living things. And not only buffalo. Other game were being driven from lands taken over by the westward-pushing wave of homesteaders, shot, poisoned and exterminated.

There were two sides to every question, and when red men, whether for sport or rendered desperate by privation and injustic, slaughtered settlers, that was a matter for concern. But the army, its outposts scattered thinly across half a continent, was charged with the preservation of order, the keeping of the peace. In theory, there was an even-handed application of justice to red men and white alike.

Some men who commanded tried hard to be fair,

to protect the rights of both sides. But there were too many others, men like Sergeant O'Reilly, whose notions of fairness McChesney found a travesty. Even the best of them had a difficult time trying to be fair.

McChesney had fought through the war with one goal in mind: the preservation of the Union. Other goals, however humanitarian, had been secondary. But in the end he had applauded the freeing of the slaves. A man was a man, regardless of the color of his skin. To treat one as an animal became in the long run as demeaning to the master as to the slave.

After he had accepted a lowered rank and service along the frontier, some of those illusions had remained. It was better amicably and legally to settle disputes between wandering tribes and the on-sweeping tide of immigrants than for both sides to slaughter senselessly. And the sole chance for the red man to survive at all, though he could not be expected to see or understand, was to accept the bitter compromise of the reservations, the guarantee of supervision and protection from the government.

But when men entered into a compact, honor was required on both sides. To cheat even in the wording or terms of a treaty, as happened all too often, was grimly prophetic of cheating to follow.

Certainly there was provocation on both sides, but the Indian, cheated in the delivery, quantity and quality of promised rations, was not much to be blamed for straying and hunting. Yet that was usually misunderstood, often deliberately, becoming an excuse for punishment out of all proportion to the offense.

Such punishment was in theory a discipline, but McChesney had seen that it was too often designed to nullify treaties, so that fresh waves of white settlers could seize desirable land, giving nothing in return, or settle the account with bullets.

The truth was that he was fed up, disillusioned. On this ride he had found but one thing to be thankful for. They were too few in numbers to fight or chastise, the roaming redskins too numerous. That sort of balance might prevent a slaughter which he found not merely abhorrent but often unjustified.

His thoughts continued to be introspective. He had liked the army; over the years it had become a way of life, grinding, hard, unrewarding in many respects, but with a companionship, even a fellowship, to be found nowhere else. On such scouts as this, the long nights under the stars, with new horizons beyond every hill—

It might be hard to explain to those who had never tasted its joys, but he had liked it. And he'd miss it, once he left it forever behind.

This would be his last scout. He'd had a letter from Martha, his sister; Martha, five years his junior, and the last of his immediate family. He was a little surprised that Martha had not married; she'd soon be reaching the age where brows would raise and whispers hiss cattishly behind her back, accusing her of being an old maid. Which was surprising, for Martha, when last he'd seen her three years before, had been a sweetly eager maid, strikingly beautiful, albeit independent-minded.

That trait was exemplified by her informing him that she was taking train and stage west, to see something of the country while the frontier remained fresh and unspoiled, to visit him at Fort Lookout, and then—she hoped—to accompany him home to the Jersey shore.

Their Uncle Tom's mill, gradually transformed into a woodworking and manufacturing enterprise, had survived the war, despite the doldrums. Since then it had prospered. And Uncle Tom remembered how young Mike had liked the smell of shavings and sawdust, the aptitude he had displayed in the year he'd served an apprenticeship, before the war had called.

The mill was prospering, and Uncle Tom was old and tired. He wanted Mike to return, to take over the management. Very soon, if he did, everything would go to the two of them, Martha and Mike. For her sake as much as his own, the old mill required an able administrator.

The prospect of seeing Martha again, of showing her the country, of really becoming acquainted, was exciting. He would not have approved her coming, with the threat of trouble like smoke over the prairie, but since she would soon be there, he was delighted.

These latter years had brought disillusionment. The buffalo were being exterminated, and so were the Indians. It was at once a case of necessity and an injustice, and like many another, Mike could perceive and possibly protest, but he could do next to nothing. He would be glad to get away rather than witness the even grimmer stages of inevitable tragedy.

His enlistment would be up within a matter of days, as Martha had remembered or learned. And Uncle Tom's offer was too generous to resist. He'd go back with her.

He glanced around, eyes narrowing. A hill rose at the side, a high, shaggy bluff, brush along its borders. Outlined upon its crest was a slender figure, watching them. McChesney heard the click as a hammer was eared back, a rifle cocked. He jerked about in time to see the long barrel of the lifting gun, the spurt of smoke jerked from its muzzle, while a thunderclap rang in his ears. Trooper Anthony, without orders, was amusing himself at target practice.

It was a long shot, doubly difficult for a man on horseback. But Anthony was either skilled or lucky. Even as the echoes rolled across the land to bounce off the bluff, the figure outlined at its top pitched and fell as loosely as a discarded scarecrow.

2.

A hush, like the calm at the eye of a hurricane, succeeded the gun blast. Shock gripped the spectators, as much because of the casualness of the killing as for its senseless brutality. McChesney had a double sense of outrage, for this was an intolerable flouting of discipline.

Yet, considering who had fired the shot, it was really not too startling. McChesney had found his attention called to the man on half a dozen occasions since the scout had begun. Too young to have served in the war, Anthony was a hulking figure, using his strength to push others around. Apparently he had gotten away with such bullying conduct all his life. McChesney had seen the pattern too often to mistake it. Finally overreaching, such men scuttled to take refuge in the military, then, shielded behind the uniform, reverted to old habits.

Mike rounded on him, a lash in his voice.

"Who gave you permission to shoot? And what, may I ask, was your notion?"

Anthony was briefly taken aback. A widening grin of satisfaction at the quality of his marksmanship lost some of its smugness.

"Why, I—the red devil was watchin' us, wan't he? That'll stop them carryin' word back, learn' em to quit spyin'."

Major Overton had dropped back to the rear. Now, as the column ground to a sudden halt, he came galloping up. Mike swung to him.

"Trooper Anthony was buying trouble, sir. That shot was murderous as well as uncalled for."

He expected, if not a word of agreement, at least a nod. Overton sat silent, and he was forced to go on.

"Of course the Indian was watching—and with reason enough, seeing such a column and not knowing the reason. He must have had what had been defined as a justifiable apprehension."

"But he was an Indian," Overton observed.

"Of course, sir. But a man fully in the open is not spying, and murder is not mere indefensible, but its consequences may prove far-reaching. In the end it could destroy all of us."

Overton heard him out, the look in his eyes more quizzical than angry. McChesney saw the sharpened attention of the others; a regard neither as impersonal nor as respectful as was customary toward an officer. Surprise was on some faces; on others, disdain or open contempt at his indignation.

They were not surprised at Anthony's impulsiveness and certainly not shocked or displeased. Clearly such a killing was no more than an accident, almost commonplace. Why should he fuss about the killing of a wild Indian?

Major Overton pulled at his mustache. The reproof in his head-shake was clearly as much for the officer as for the soldier.

"Why now, no doubt you're right, Mr. McChesney. The trooper may have been a shade over-hasty. Still and all, it was a good shot, and other skulkers who may have witnessed it will have reason to think twice before incurring the army's displeasure."

His glance shifted to O'Reilly, his tone sharpening. "Why are we halted? Move ahead."

Clearly the matter was at an end, the affair rated as an incident, no more. The reprimand had been for McChesney. A grin replaced the momentary uncertainty on Anthony's face. McChesney clamped his own jaws in incredulity and dismay.

A part of his surprise was caused by the fact that a man noted for strict, even harsh discipline would take such a tone before his men; in essence, it amounted to holding an officer up to contempt, and that was contrary to the rules. Yet such action as Anthony's was by no means uncommon. Life all along the frontier was cheaply held—especially the lives of men whose skin was of another color.

And Overton was clearly as indifferent to the possible consequences of such an act as was the trooper.

There was another reaction which was even more frightening. It applied to the men of both companies, and was increasingly apparent as they put their horses to a trot. McChesney had seen such a manifestation too many times to be mistaken. Wolves might slink timidly while alone, but when they were drawing together in a pack, closing about a victim, the lust for blood overcame their apprehension, transforming them into killers.

Two-footed animals, given the occasion, behaved similarly.

The scent of blood stirred latent savagery. Soliders, in the end, had only one reason for being. Their training had but one objective. Properly disciplined, kept under restraint, they were an effective instrument for maintaining law and order. But as with a savage watchdog, once the leash was slipped, they had the instincts of the pack. Men could be too well trained in the business of killing.

Overton had requested McChesney's transfer to his command because he was an expert on Indians. That seemed to have been forgotten.

Well, this was not his responsibility, and he was increasingly tired of it all. Once they were back at Lookout and his enlistment was up, he'd take his leave, with fewer regrets than he'd once believed possible.

Sergeant O'Reilly was dropping back. His eyes met

McChesney's in a bland, expressionless stare, but the quirk at the corners of his mouth bespoke his pleasure at the turn of events.

Overton fell in alongside. He removed his hat, clutching it with the hand which held the bridle reins, leaving his other hand free to fish out a blue bandana and mop dust and perspiration from his face. He replaced the hat, and his tone was as warm, as pleasant as the day.

"It's a chore, such riding, but necessary. We have to keep a watch to mount a show of strength, to show the flag. That is a soldier's life. At least it breaks the tedium of endless drills, of the parade ground and the same horizon stretching beyond the stockade, until its monotony sours the spirit."

"That's true enough," McChesney concurred. "On the whole, the trail is closer to the needs of a man."

Overton smiled. Beneath his mustache, big teeth flashed white and strong.

"Well, we've both had a lot of soldiering and someone must do it. On balance, I suppose it's as good a career as most. I could never be a banker, for instance, or sell cheese or shoes from behind a counter. Yet I suppose those who follow such lines find the life satisfying, preferring the peace of their existence, a peace which we work to procure for them."

"Viewed that way, sir, this life has its rewards."

"Without such, it would be untenable. But I suppose we'll die in harness; perhaps even in bed, though that seems unlikely. More likely with our boots on—and, hopefully, with our hair on."

"That was the way I had expected to die—until recently," McChesney conceded. This might be a good time to break the news that he was leaving the service, that his enlistment would soon be up. It was the fair and courteous thing to forewarn the commandant.

Overton's eyebrows rose. "Do you mean that you're thinking of leaving the service after all these years?"

"I have two good reasons. An uncle who has built up a good business, which he is no longer able to operate, wants me to take it over for my sister and myself. She is the other, perhaps greater reason. She is on her way West by now, I presume, intending to visit the fort, to see the country and what the life is like. But she wants me to accompany her home."

A surprised whistle escaped the major. He turned to regard McChesney more fully.

"Good reasons, indeed! My congratulations! And your sister—I take it that she is your junior?"

"By several years. I expect she may leave a trail of broken hearts among the younger officers."

"In making such a supposition you could scarcely be called a gambling man. But you are not so old, Lieutenant—nor am I, for that matter. It's true that we're old hands at this game, at wars and the rumors of war. But you will have time for a full life in your new career."

"If its boredom, or the memory of this, permits, or if we return in safety from this sweep."

The eyebrows lifted like humping caterpillars.

"You don't anticipate anything untoward, surely?"

"I hope not. But the tribes are restless, and it's increasingly evident that the feeling extends to nearly every tribe or wandering group of hunters."

"Why, that's true enough," the major granted. "I'm of the opinion that more of the plaguey devils are off their reservations than on—using the pretext of hunting against the needs of winter. But we won't ride almost defenseless for long. I hadn't told you, but we'll be touching at Fort Norris, where we'll be substantially reinforced. For that I am duly thankful. From all reports, there is a considerable gathering of Cheyennes somewhere in the vicinity of the Two Buttes, with perhaps some Arapahoes and very possibly others in the vicinity. If it is their thought to test us, or perhaps to intimidate us—well, that is a game which two can play."

McChesney listened without any change of expression. As though regretting the incident of the trooper, the major was going out of his way to be amiable, to inform him of matters on which he had been left to guess or speculate. Such reports as the scouts had brought in, Overton had kept to himself.

"Two Buttes?" McChesney repeated, envisioning

the country. He had ridden across it nearly two years before. "That sounds reasonable. The Cheyenne have long made it a sort of headquarters when they are in this section, and there is good hunting in the vicinity."

"Perhaps good hunting for several sorts of game," Overton said drily. "And that is a good reason it may be better if they are not forewarned of our coming— as spies might like to do."

That was clearly a reference to the killing of the watcher from the butte top, an extenuation for what Trooper Anthony had done. McChesney studied the man beside him anew, keeping his own face carefully blank. Could it be that, despite his years of service, Overton knew so little of Indians as to believe that the watcher had been there to spy and would do so openly, or that the unseen eyes which certainly watched them were not there, merely because they kept out of sight? And yet there were officers, all too often in positions of command, whose naivete both bewildered and shocked him.

"Which reminds me," Overton added. "Our scouts don't know that country very well, so we need a really competent guide. I understand that there's a man in the vicinity who might fill the bill, name of Sibley."

McChesney made to speak, but thought better of it. He was learning fast not only about this company of cavalry, but about its commander. If Overton wanted such information as McChesney was supposed to be along to give, he'd ask for it.

He was partly right as regarded Sibley. Black Eagle Sibley certainly knew the country and had the qualifications of an excellent guide. But whether he would be willing to serve in that capacity, under existing circumstances, was another matter. He was getting along in years, and might prefer, with colder weather close at hand, to crouch over the fire in his own tepee, his wants ministered to by his squaw. Those would be easier than the exigencies of the trail.

Even more potent a reason, Sibley was a half-breed—the son of a fugitive black slave and an Indian mother; a Cheyenne mother, if McChesney's memory and information were correct. As such, he was a Cheyenne, and might not care to guide an expedition whose members took pot shots at Indians who trustingly exposed themselves, and whose purpose they must now gravely doubt.

Overton's next words confirmed that he knew all about Sibley, from other sources. He beckoned to O'Reilly, where the sergeant rode just out of earshot.

"I have a mission for you, O'Reilly," he said as the sergeant came up. "I believe that you know about this nigger Indian called Black Eagle Sibley?"

A look of anticipation touched O'Reilly's lips, then was gone again.

"Black Sibley? I've heard of him."

"Our present scouts should at least be able to locate him for you. You will take three men in all, and find him as quickly as possible. Do so unobtrusively, so as to cause no alarm. Make sure that he is not forewarned of your coming, so as to be able to skip out or escape. We want him for a guide."

"Yes sir. And if he should wish to refuse?"

"We need him in condition to guide us. I think you understand, Sergeant."

3.

Overton caught McChesney's glance, speculative and wholly sober, and a flush mounted in the major's cheeks as though he had been detected in mischief. He opened his mouth, then closed it without speaking. Somehow, McChesney seemed to place him in the wrong. Like O'Reilly he understood the order.

The conscription of civilians had officially ended years before. But such a technicality could not be permitted to stand in the way when the army wanted something.

Again, Overton swung alongside.

"What do you know about this Sibley?" he asked. "I've heard a lot of conflicting reports."

"I understand that his father was an escaped slave," McChesney returned. "He lived with the Cheyennes and married a squaw. Black Eagle has always been counted a full-fledged member of the tribe, but as a mixed blood he's caught in the middle—pulled first one way and then the other. His sympathies are of course with the Indians, but I understand that he lives pretty much by himself, in a cabin rather than a tepee, preferring civilized customs to savage ones."

Overton was incredulous. "But what would he know of that? I've seen slave shanties—" He shrugged.

"I suspect that it's a case of trying to live up to a dream. Every man has to have his dream. Without one, what is there to live for?"

Such a philosophy, with its implication that red or black men could aspire even as whites did, was beyond Overton. He dismissed it with a shrug.

"But he knows the country, I take it?"

"Better than most, probably. But he's getting along in years, and would probably prefer to sit by the fire instead of taking the field."

"So would I," Overton said shortly. "We can't always have what we want. And it's easier and a lot less trouble when we can find these renegades in their camps instead of having to hunt them down."

"Why do either?" McChesney countered. "Sure, some of them are off the reservation, but only to hunt. They'll head back of their own accord as soon as the snow flies, and there'll be less trouble all around."

"My orders are to round them up and herd them back. You know the reason for that as well as I. We can't allow them to run as they please, whenever and wherever their fancy leads. There are too many settlers in the middle of those old hunting grounds."

And that, of course, was the crux. It was useless to point out that many if not most of those settlers were pre-empting land reserved for the Indians by treaties, so that the Indians felt themselves to be within the letter as well as the spirit of the law. To suggest that the interlopers instead be rounded up and moved off would be a waste of breath. But for the moment at least, the major's thoughts seemed to coincide with his.

"That might be the fair thing to do," he said explosively: "to clear out the whites who are trespassing. Only instead of having on our hands one war against the redskins, we'd have two wars—and no backing from headquarters. One at a time is all that I can handle."

O'Reilly had carried out his orders. He was waiting when they caught up the next day, along with Black Eagle Sibley. Born a Cheyenne, Sibley had found contentment as a warrior through most of his life. Growing older, he had become given to thought and introspection, intensified by the freeing of his father's people. A fact which he had long accepted he had come to ponder and take pride in—that his deeper color was something of which to be proud.

Gradually he had reverted to being a black man, living apart, as aloof as possible from interracial quarrels and conflicts. Once he had been a magnificent physical specimen. Now he was wasted, twisted by disease, his voice muted. Standing passively, he eyed his captors without hope.

"Yassuh, Major, I knows the country," he agreed. "Ought to, after riding ovah it fo' a lifetime. Only trouble is, I'm that creaky in the j'ints an' stove up all ovah, I cain't sca'cely set a horse no more. Ain' no good to myse'f, no good to nobody."

"If you fall off, we'll pick you up," Overton assured him. "You won't have to worry."

The old man showed a flash of the courage which had made him a great warrior, even while differentiating himself from his associates.

"The Indians always treated me good, even if mah pappy come among 'em as a stranger. Be kind of a treach'ous trick to lead an ahmy against them, an' them all unsuspectin'."

"We're only going to round them up and herd them back where they belong." Overton explained, and he might have been talking of a herd of cattle. "And in any case, we'll find them."

"Yassuh, I reckon likely. Only if they saw me leadin' you, they'd figure everything was right an' friendly. I sho' wouldn't feel right misleadin' them, suh."

The major's patience snapped.

"I don't have to argue. Either you serve us as a scout, or we'll hang you from that cottonwood yonder."

Sibley's gaze did not falter before the bluster,

though he knew Overton by reputation.

"Might be better. But I'll ride along," he accepted.

That evening, above the embers of a cook-fire, Overton questioned him more particularly.

"I have information that a considerable number of Cheyennes are camped in the vicinity of Two Buttes. What do you know about that?"

Sibley nodded. "Reckon so, Major. Old-time huntin' camp, from way back. Not too good no more, with a road cuttin' past and wagons an' stages scarin' the game away. But the squaws an' children keep the camp, an' the hunters range far."

"How many women and children?"

"All of 'em. An' when they're along, then the braves ain' fixin' to cause no trouble."

Overton did not argue the point. "I'm also informed that quite a few of the Arapahoes are with them. Isn't that rather unusual?"

Sibley shrugged.

"My pappy tell me how his Ol' Massa make a comment one time, when a big 'lection campaign was ragin', with to'chlight parades an' bar'ls of whiskey. He remark how politics make some mighty strange bedfellows."

"He was certainly right. And you're saying that life-long enemies are banding together now to battle white men?"

"No suh, I ain' quite say that. They ain' fixin' to fight, not less'n they's drove to it. But when whites keep crowdin', shovin'—'gainst both of 'em—yassuh, I 'spect likely there's some 'Pahoes thereabouts."

"And maybe others? Dakotahs, Nez Percés, Crows?"

Sibley shook a patient head.

"I wouldn't know, suh. Could be, only I doubt it."

"Well, we'll find out. Anyhow, Two Buttes is our destination."

Night was closing, but sufficient light lingered so they could pick out the horses at graze on picket, the men grouped about the fading embers of cooking fires. Sibley's glanced ranged, speculatively, but he merely nodded.

"Yassuh."

"And we could be sticking our heads into a noose, so few against so many," Overton added slyly. "Did you have that in mind, maybe, you black devil?"

A flicker shone in the old man's eyes; otherwise he gave no sign of resentment.

"No suh, Major. You ridin' peaceful, they huntin' peaceful—no reason fo' no trouble."

"There won't be, by the time we get there," Overton assured him. "We're swinging past Fort Norris, where we'll receive reinforcements—heavy reinforcements. Captain Schmitt is to join us there, with Companies H and R, both at full strength."

"Yassuh, Major. Sho'ly, suh."

Reinforcements in such numbers would completely alter the complexion of the expedition. From a supposed scouting sweep, it acquired war-like overtones.

"I just thought you'd like to know." Overton's tone was sardonic. "And it's perhaps just as well that you're too stove up for much walking or riding. Anyone who tried to sneak away and reach them with a warning would be shot like a coyote."

Two companies at full strength would of course be fully officered. McChesney knew of Captain Schmitt by reputation. He was precisely the sort that Overton would prefer to work with: a man well fitted for the sort of duty which might devolve upon him.

Fort Norris was a misnomer. It was little more than an outpost, vulnerable to attack should trouble erupt or flame spread across the frontier. To McChesney's mind, that was a possibility which they were encouraging by their present course. The word would be spreading far faster than they could travel, and almost every letter would carry ominous overtones.

The Indian leadership, in the aggregate, sought to control impatient young warriors, to adjust, however painfully, to living alongside whites, to peace. In their hearts, nearly every chief was opposed to conciliation, but in their heads was the sober realization that for every white man they might kill, ten or even a hundred would take his place. War under such circumstances, however justified, could lead only to their extermination.

Others assessed their plight more hopefully. If all the tribes who once had warred upon each other would join against the common foe, they would have at least a chance of winning. Such a possibility was better than dying by slower, more painful methods—starvation, disease, cold or massacre.

The situation had grown unchancy, looming darkly in the minds of red and white alike; a matter of life or death, as delicately triggered as the jaws of a steel trap.

Schmitt and his companies were waiting for them, and they had come upon buffalo, a few remnants of vanished herds. There was feasting.

At the banquet, McChesney met his new fellow-officers. Of them, he felt most drawn to Bentley, a second lieutenant, new alike to the army and such a life and, surprisingly, a young man. Most officers of whatever rank were beginning to show their age; there was a surfeit of them left over from the war, still hopeful of continuing a military career.

Bentley was the exception. A yellow-haired giant with a wide sunny smile, he rode with stars in his eyes.

Overton was in an excellent mood as they lined out the next morning. Now they were in sufficient force to intimidate an enemy, or fight, whichever might be necessary. It was increasingly clear to McChesney that, like Schmitt and Carrington and many others, Overton would prefer direct action. Convinced in his own mind that it had to come, he was impatient for a showdown which would get it over with.

"We can teach them a lesson, if necessary," he observed complacently. "These are all seasoned troops. But it shouldn't come to anything beyond a possible skirmish or so. When they see our numbers, they'll know what we can do. So we should be able to swing past the Buttes, throw the fear of the Lord into them, and go on back to Lookout. And I'm doubly anxious to make it back without delay."

He grinned at McChesney. Mike had the strange feeling that personally the major liked him, even while disapproving of certain of his attitudes.

"Your sister is on her way there, you tell me, and having such a lady as our guest will be a welcome break in the routine. But she won't be the only one. There's another lady coming to visit—also young and charming, whose acquaintance I was privileged to make more than a year ago when on business farther to the East. Miss Margaret Trout. You will have met her father, or at least you'll know of him. Colonel Malcolm Trout."

"I never had the pleasure of meeting him, but he has a great reputation."

"And a great daughter. The two of them, Maggie and your sister, should enliven our usually dull society. I'm certainly looking forward to it."

As they moved, the way had grown increasingly

rough and broken. A horse stumbled and went down, throwing its rider. McChesney saw that it was Sibley, lying unstirring, his arms outflung.

Overton's good humor vanished as suddenly as the accident had occurred. The old man would be of no further use as a scout.

"Leave him," Overton said callously. "He didn't want to come anyhow."

4.

Carried out, that order would amount to a death sentence. Then, catching McChesney's incredulous glance, Overton colored and amended it.

"He'd be no loss. But load him on his horse again."

His tone suggested that the original order had been a joke, but McChesney was not convinced. Sibley was too frail and weak for the task for which he had been unwillingly drafted. Overton's viewpoint was that when a man ceased to be useful, he was not worth bothering with.

Once he was hoisted to the saddle, it was necessary to tie him there. It was hardly a kindness and could be a mistake. Aside from that single watcher on the hilltop, none of the Indians had shown themselves, but McChesney had no doubt that they were being kept under observation. To the eyes of a distant wacther, it might seem that the old Eagle was a prisoner.

Such an indignity would increase their resentment. But either that possibility did not occur to Overton, or he was too busy with another problem to bother. As Sibley had tried to tell them, he had been too old and ill for the hardships of the trail, and again they needed a scout. He talked it over with Schmitt.

"I'd prefer a Pawnee. They hate the Cheyennes, but that's an asset under these conditions. And they probably hate us worse, so I don't know where we'd find one."

"I wouldn't trust one even as far as I could keep him in my sights," Schmitt returned. "But have you thought of the McGillicuddys? I'm told that they've done some good work in the past."

"I know about them," Overton admitted grimly. "A squaw man, with a mongrel brood. And they not only hate whites, but count themselves as Cheyennes, like their mother. How could you trust them?"

Schmitt's smile was cat-like.

"The old man could serve as a hostage, if necessary. It's not far out of our way to swing past their ranch."

To Schmitt's bewilderment, his suggestion was viewed with disfavor.

"It might be effective, but I don't like it. The old man—they call him The McGillicuddy—is a white man. I understand that he was born and reared in Glasgow."

"Likely enough, since he has a Scottish name. But what's wrong with that?"

"There's a difference between a white man and an

Indian," Overton said simply.

Schmitt was disdainful.

"In my opinion, sir, a squaw man forfeits the right to be regarded as white. I'd class him as no better than his mongrel progeny or their mother."

"I understand your viewpoint, Captain, but I can't fully agree. Some Indian woman are rather attractive, and it has also been good business for a trader or rancher to establish an alliance with the tribes. Not that I approve, but I can understand."

"I can't," Schmitt said flatly. "But in any case, the conditions would appear to strengthen my argument."

"We'll do it," Overton decided. "Circumstances warrant action, however drastic. We should be able to make an abrupt change of course and drop in on them before they expect us."

At the proper time the line of march was altered. Schmitt was pleased, while at the same time contemptuous of his superior. He had heard quite a lot about Orlando Overton and had looked forward to serving under him. Their notions regarding law and order on the frontier, as well as the proper way to deal with Indians, had seemed to run along similar lines. Now he saw that Overton entertained certain ideas which might turn out to be hindrances, had unjustified qualms that could interfere with necessary action.

Overton seemed to be battling with a conflict of

conscience, trying to justify harsh measures. A strong man should sweep scruples aside. Even to discuss a course of action with subordinates, arguing the pros and cons, could be a fatal weakness, while to make a distinction between a squaw man and a white man was even worse.

In one sense he was correct. Alexander McGilli-cuddy was a name to conjure with in that country. He had come as a trapper and trader, then had turned to raising stock, bringing up one of the first herds from Texas. Since he was allied with the powerful and dominant Cheyennes, no questions had arisen about his taking as much land as his dreams might encompass, and there probably was no other man, red or white, of comparable wealth and power. He had the backing of a tough and competent crew, and the warriors of more than one tribe would respond should he call for help.

In Schmitt's mind, that was not a risk but an asset. None of the tribes could challenge such a force as now marched, and if they made the mistake of trying, so much the better. On one point he was assured that he and the major saw eye to eye. The more Indians they killed on this sweep, the fewer would remain to plague them in the future.

They timed their arrival at the ranch for its ultimate effect. Swinging at dusk, they marched an extra hour, then pitched camp with their objective almost in view. Astir long before the usual time,

the army moved purposefully through the still heavy
gloom. They reached the sprawling cluster of ranch
buildings just as the cook, the only equally early
riser, was beating a raucous tattoo on an iron triangle
to arouse the rest of the crew. Still sleepy-eyed with
bewilderment, the cowboys blinked in disbelief at
the seemingly endless horde of invading horsemen.

The surprise was as complete as Overton had
hoped, though not quite as satisfactory. Alex Mc-
Gillicuddy, a patriarchal figure at seventy, full-
bearded but no longer formidable, they found in his
bed, cursing a broken leg sustained from a falling
horse a couple of days before. The distinction was
vital. He had not been thrown. His horse had put
its foot in a gopher hole and gone down.

Young Axel and Gavin were absent; whether they
were on ranch business or perhaps riding with the
Cheyennes, of whom they considered themselves full
tribal members, neither Alexander nor James, his
second son, bothered to explain. James, at thirty,
was a physical replica of his father, minus the beard,
though with a ruddier cast of countenance. Overton
explain to him his wish that he accompany the army
as guide and scout.

The request was considered in a hostile silence.
Alexander McGillicuddy flung a question.

"Whereat might ye be headin', the noo? And for
how long?"

"I'm informed that there's a considerable gathering of braves in the vicinity of Two Buttes," Overton explained. "We prefer to break it up before trouble develops."

"And ye'd break it up with bullets, not words," Alex McGillicuddy had never been a man to mince words, and he saw no reason to begin now. "You have that reputation, Major Overton—as does Captain Schmitt. A reputation, ma mannie," he added, with a relapse into his boyhood brogue, "that stinks!"

Angry blood coursed in Schmitt's face, giving it a darker hue than that of the younger McGillicuddy. He in turn raised his eyes to a woman who appeared at the doorway to the bedroom, an unspoken appeal in her dark eyes. She was a fine figure of a woman, and again Overton could find excuses for Alex McGillicuddy taking a wife from among the natives.

That the high anger of his father coursed in James McGillicuddy's veins was not to be doubted, but it was tempered by a poise and wisdom inherited from his mother's side. He met her look, glancing from the window in the brightening day at the overwhelming force arrayed against them, and made his decision.

"I can spare the time to ride as far as Two Buttes, if that is your wish, Major. You are right as to the gathering, but it is only a hunting expedition, with more women and children than men. They seek no trouble."

"But can as much be said for these? I dinna like

it, boy," his father protested. "'Tis too strong a
force by far, Major, to have a peaceful intent."

Overton disdained making a denial. He was already drawing on his gloves.

"Then the sooner we are on our way, the better.
I trust that you will enjoy a speedy recovery, sir."

The McGillicuddy snorted.

"'Tis dom little ye care," he returned. "And still
less do I care for your empty mouthings!"

They stalked from the house. The ranch crew,
having observed them, had gone in to breakfast, a not
too subtle gesture of contempt. James McGillicuddy,
passing up his own meal, his mouth hard-set, selected
a powerful roan cayuse from the remuda in one of
three adjoining corrals. He roped and saddled it,
tied a blanket and slicker behind the saddle, thrust
a rifle into the saddle sheath and swung up.

"I'm ready," he said shortly.

Schmitt made as if to speak, but closed his lips at
Overton's warning glance. The long column moved.

McChesney, having caught Schmitt's considering
glance on the cross-bar from which the triangle of
iron was suspended, could guess what the captain
had intended to say: that the younger McGillicuddy
was showing sense. If he had not, his father would
by now be suspended like the triangle from the
cross-bar.

Overton rode in an increasing anger, made worse
by the fact that it was directed as much against him-

self as against others. These actions were necessary,
and Schmitt was right in that he was tough-minded
enough to take whatever moves necessity might require. But this sweep that they were making, half
scout, half expedition, was unlike others. There had
been no real sign of trouble anywhere when they
had set out. With each day of riding, as though they
had fostered it, the atmosphere altered, like an approaching change in the weather.

The watcher from the butte had been only one of
several incidents. But such gestures were warnings
to savages who could understand nothing less—

Inexplicably, he found himself on the defensive,
forced almost against his will to consult, to explain
himself, and finding no satisfaction in the doing.

The fault lay with Lieutenant Mike McChesney,
who had offered almost no protest, but somehow had
made his feelings known beyond any shadow of
doubt. And to be bothered or influenced by the displeasure of anyone, particularly a subordinate, was
new to Overton and not at all to his liking.

The trouble, he supposed, was that McChesney
had been a high-ranking officer at one time, and
Overton could not fail to regard him as an equal.
McChesney's career had been at least as distin-
guished as his own, with flashes of brilliance—a quality which Overton secretly realized was lacking in
his. It was ridiculous, but he craved this man's good
opinion, while realizing that each act which he was

compelled to engage in served further to lower any regard which McChesney might originally have felt.

He could assert his authority, and if need be would, but there were times when that gave him no satisfaction; indeed, today it had been just the contrary.

This was a ride from which there could be no turning back. Moreover, he would do things his own way, not McChesney's. He was the commander, and he had the courage of his convictions. For McChesney's notions he had only contempt.

But the fact remained, like the rawness of a saddle sore, hidden under a blanket but with the festering constantly painful, that he liked not only his job but himself less and less. The certain knowledge that he was riding on a course hell-bent for destruction contained no comfort.

Black Eagle Sibley they had left behind at the ranch. Whether he would live or not was a moot question, for the trip had been hard on him. But McGillicuddy's woman would give him the best of care. Overton snorted at his twist of mind. He was actually terming her the old Scotsman's woman rather than a squaw.

Jim McGillicuddy, Bentley and McChesney had been riding ahead since midday. McChesney came galloping back, pulling up to report.

"There's a small encampment in the gulch beyond that brush, sir. Not more than half a dozen lodges, and with the look of a poor lot. Clearly peaceful. Probably women and children, at least for the most part."

Overton knew what he was actually saying: that they would do better to swing a little and leave such a camp untroubled. Anger roweled him like the lance of a spur. Because McChesney was right, his perverse temper surged to the fore.

"We'll have a look," he instructed shortly. "It never pays to take chances."

5.

The three had come together naturally, riding in advance of the others, alert for possible trouble—McChesney, Bentley and James McGillicuddy. Lieutenant Bentley, the last arrival, seemed somewhat uncertain as he joined them.

"I hope I'm not intruding," he apologized. "I'm pretty much of a greenhorn at this sort of thing, and perhaps I can pick up a few pointers if I ride with a pair of experts."

"I'm sure I have no objections." Jim's voice was tight, like his manner. He was accompanying the expedition under duress and was justifiably resentful. Then, as though sensing Bentley's craving for companionship and something more, he eyed the class ring on the latter's finger, where his ungloved hand rested lightly on the saddle-horn. "So you're a Harvard man, too?"

Bentley looked surprised. Then he saw the ring on McGillicuddy's finger and flushed with pleasure.

"Why yes, I am. It's unusual to find another out

here—I mean—"

"I'm half Indian, and this is an uncivilized country," Jim supplied. "Don't be afraid to say it. But there are degrees of savagery. From what I've learned of Scottish history, it strikes me that the old Lairds of the Highlands were never so happy as when battling the English or, denied that pleasure, bickering among themselves. Once the bonnie benefits of peace were imposed upon them, they stagnated, or their blood grew overheated, as was the case with my father. He took ship for a far country, then followed the sun on its long swing to a still more distant sea. His heart was torn between the shining mountains which towered above his own highlands, and these vasty plains. But having found my mother here, in her land he abode."

Bentley eyed him with surprise and increasing respect. Here was no untutored savage, but a gentleman from his own school, one who viewed the world with the eyes of a dreamer and spoke with the accents of a poet.

McChesney concealed his own amusement. Lieutenant Bentley was discovering that the gift of eloquence was not a heritage reserved exclusively to any one race of men, tribe or color.

"Had I been consulted, nothing could have pleased me better," Jim went on. "I never knew the highlands or the Rockies, but this land and people satisfied all my requirements. Too much so, perhaps.

My father remembered his own heritage and felt that I should know something about it. As boys, my brothers and myself were well tutored. How it came about I never quite learned, the man being reticent concerning himself, but an Englishman drifted into camp. He was a stray on trouble's range, frail, already looking toward a gathering sunset from an advanced stage of tuberculosis. He had drifted over the range unharmed, those who might have coveted his scalp perhaps taking pity on him. Or what they say may have applied: That the Lord looks out for fools and tenderfeet.

"Not that he was ignorant; merely foolish in certain respects. My father took him in, and he tutored us, Alex, Gavin and myself, to such good purpose that, for all their astonishment, at the college they felt constrained to admit me. Alex and Gavin would have none of it, so it fell to me to please the Laird."

He dropped the subject, as though everything had been said. Between the three, riding together, an understanding developed. However oddly assorted, they were birds of a common feather.

Their discovery of the scraggly encampment near the bottom of a long easy gulch came as a surprise. McChesney made his own estimate. Wanderers—a small party who had strayed. And even in this season when the hunters laid in meat against the winter's needs, they remained on the brink of starvation. There were such among red men as well as

white, well-meaning but improvident, following th
gleam of a faulty star, never quite attaining thei
goal.

A handful of wanderers lived precariously in mor
ways than one. But most others, even among tribe
normally hostile, were inclined to pity them and t
refrain from attack, placing no undue obstacles i
their way. More often than not such folks were re
garded as under the protection of spirits.

Apparently this group had strayed among people
alien to them. Otherwise they would not be so clos
to a far larger encampment. From the crest of th
coulee he was unsure of their tribe. They woul
be neither Cheyenne nor Arapahoe, almost sure?
not Sioux.

The same puzzlement was in McGillicuddy's eye
as he studied them.

"Among cattle, down Texas way, they call then
mavericks," he murmured. "How they contrive t
exist is a wonder." That was the white man in hin
speaking. Then the Indian took over, and h
shrugged.

"But does not the Good Book say that the Lor
looks after His own?" He frowned back at the ap
proaching column of soldiers, then at his companions
For all his philosophy, worry was in the glance.

"They've nothing to fear from the people of th
plains. But will the major understand? Or Captai
Schmitt? Schmitt has a reputation which outrun

him—as does the scent of a skunk."

McChesney nodded his understanding. "Some do not understand," he agreed, "at times from ignorance."

"Which is scarcely as bad as wilfulness. They're heading right this way—"

Again McChesney followed his line of thought. They could not report back and suggest altering the line of march without giving a logical reason. Almost anything would arouse Overton's suspicion. Yet if the army came suddenly upon the camp, with or without warning—

In the eyes of the army, an Indian encampment was an Indian encampment. Overton and Schmitt would readily distinguish between a homestead on the prairie, a village or a town; so, too, would they distinguish between Yankee and German, English and Swede. All were different, but white.

But to them all colored men, red, black or yellow, alone or *en masse*, were alike. And because they lacked the perception to see any difference, to them it did not exist.

"I'll ride back and report," McChesney said. "I was brought along for my supposed knowledge."

"Which can be unwelcome when it runs counter to inclination," Jim murmured.

His report given, McChesney held his shoulders stiffly against a shrug of disappointment at Overton's swiftly contrary decision. It was what he had ex-

pected, though he had made it plain that the group
was peaceful, posing no threat.

Riding back, flanked by Overton and Schmitt, he
sensed the flaring excitement in them and in those
who rode behind. Even the nostrils of the ponies were
distended as they sensed the contagion. Wild beasts
could smell blood a long way off.

And so, at times, could men.

McGillicuddy glanced at Mike, then added his
own conclusions as the officers drew up.

"They seem to be a small bunch who have run
into hard luck—harmless and certainly peaceful, but
probably lazy."

"All Indians are shiftless," Schmitt pronounced
dogmatically. McGillicuddy's head jerked, the hot
blood flooding his face. Then he clamped his lips.

"If I might venture a suggestion, sir—" McChesney
strove to ease the tension— "perhaps Mr. McGillicuddy and I could ride into the camp, parley then
report back—"

"You might have done that half an hour ago and
not wasted time," Schmitt interjected. His glance
ranged over the campsite below. Smoke drifted lazily
from a single cook-fire. A dog drowsed in the shade
of a tepee. A squaw emerged from it, crossed to the
blaze, then returned inside. It was clear that no
watch was kept, nor did they have any suspicion of
danger.

Overton stared from McChesney to Schmitt, not

reproving the latter for interrupting. Schmitt pursued his advantage.

"Give me a score of men," he said. "I'll ride in and investigate."

Overton's face was briefly troubled. Here was a clash of wills; his two senior and most trusted officers were at cross-purposes. He did not agree with Mike McChesney, but he knew his record and, against his will, respected it.

Schmitt he liked because their opinions and inclinations were similar, yet somehow he distrusted, almost feared the man. Schmitt had an overriding ambition, and Overton had come to sense the danger inherent in driving too hard. But Schmitt was senior to McChesney in rank; also, he was the cutting edge to the blade which Overton might need at any time. His face tightening, he nodded.

"Permission granted, Captain."

No more than that; no instructions, no restraints. McChesney tensed as Schmitt made a swift selection of men, including a bugler. That in itself was ominous, unnecessary and out of place. This man was like Custer, impelled to do things with a flair. Like him, he was completely certain in his own mind as to the rightness of his own opinions.

Lieutenant Bentley was of the group, yet apart. He was learning fast. Disbelief and uncertainty showed in his eyes. McGillicuddy looked at McChesney, and anger, smoldering deep under craggy brows, was catching fire. But like the rest of them, he could only wait.

The fire, the excitement which had spread from man to horse and flashed along the ranks like the heat of the sun, mounted to an unseen but vibrant thunder. Schmitt formed his men, then took his place in front, sword in hand, a gallant figure. He shook his head at the inquiring glance of the bugler, then led the way, a walk increasing to a trot.

They had covered half the distance when a small boy emerged from a tent and stared upward, unbelieving. He turned with a cry, a terrified wail. Then, at Schmitt's signal, the bugle blared the charge, and the line went from a trot to a gallop.

They swept down the slope, brave in blue, hoofs drumming, pounding like war drums in answer to the bugle. The sword lifted in a slashing signal, the sun dancing along the blade.

The selected men who followed were well trained, requiring no additional instructions. Revolvers lifted, spitting venom like snakes. The roll of the guns caught up the invisible thunder in a long crash.

The hard-galloping line had spread to encompass the width of the camp. They reached the tepees, smashing across and over. Schmitt swung his horse, jerking it to a frenzied stop, leaning, and the sword was stabbing. A squaw's face lifted in agonized appeal, to vanish in a crimson smear. Wild cries shrieked alarm.

A man burst from a tepee, his stare unbelieving. He raised an arm in a frantic gesture of greeting, then altered it swiftly to the signal of peace. His other hand clutched wildly at his ragged white man's shirt.

Straightening, Schmtit bellowed an order. The bugle blared again, and the charging riders' swung around. This time nothing remained. The episode was over almost as swiftly as it had erupted. A thin smoke drifted from the scattered remnants of the fire.

A ragged cheer went up from the watching men, their ranks broken now into a loose grouping as they stared. Overton did not reprove them. The same contagion blazed in his eyes.

Then, meeting McChesney's stark glance, his own shifted. The surging color receded in his cheeks. He gave the word to O'Reilly, and at the sergeant's order, the formation was restored, and they rode orderly fashion, slowly pacing, to the bottom of the slope.

McGillicuddy's face was like stone. Bentley looked ill. This was not as he had pictured the gallantry of service. McChesney was coldly alert.

The tepees had all been flattened except for one. Though riddled with bullets, it still stood. Beside it, a squaw lay face down, having tried with her own body to shield a papoose. Like the man, even the dog, all were dead.

Something was clutched in the fingers of the man. He had tried to give a greeting of welcome, a sign of friendship. McChesney dismounted, to pluck the folded, worn paper from stiffening fingers. It was stained, but of good quality, like an official document. McChesney scanned it.

There was fancy gold lettering at the head, and the writing was in an exquisite penmanship. It gave greeting and salutation and an assurance from the War Department that Chief Little Wolf was a firm friend of the white men, under the official protection of the army and authorities of the government of the United States.

6.

Little Wolf, of the Crows. It was there in stark simplicity. The tribe had always been friendly to white men.

Silently McChesney passed the sheet to Overton, who had halted his horse alongside. The major scanned it hastily, then, his brows knitting, studied the message more carefully. A hush had succeeded the crackling of guns, a quiet broken only by a rasp of agonized breathing, the groan of a badly wounded man off at one side, partially hidden by fringing brush.

A final gunshot put a period to that, and Overton jerked, taken by surprise. He scowled as Seamus O'Reilly strode into full view, slipping a fresh cartridge into his revolver, transferring the weapon to the holster.

"What was that?" Overton rasped. His nerves were clearly on edge.

"I was putting a poor devil out of his misery," O'Reilly explained, "as I'd do for a horse or dog."

The sheet, worn and frayed, tore suddenly in Overton's gripping fingers. He eyed the remnants, scowled, then tore them again, scattering the fragments. He was still silent as Schmitt pulled alongside, gazing around with a mock regret which scarcely covered the complacency in his eyes. For an instant he stared down at the dead squaw and the child she had tried vainly to protect.

"Now that is too bad," he pronounced. "But they should have known better than to reach for weapons at our approach. Faced with such hostility, I could do nothing other than sound the charge."

Overton clutched at the excuse, obviously grateful. "I suppose it did look that way," he acknowledged. "In any case, what's done is done."

"It's a lesson for them which may prove useful," Schmitt said truculently. "The others will understand that we tolerate no nonsense."

Jim McGillicuddy had remained a spectator, looking about in a tight-lipped silence. He was of the Cheyenne, and between the Cheyennes and the Crows there was no liking. But outrage buried in his voice.

"A man could be no more wrong on both counts," he said angrily. "The lesson, as you call it, may well pass unnoticed, since they are not of the Cheyenne nor of any concern to them. Had they been, it would have aroused them to a fighting pitch. Also what, if I may ask, is the captain's definition of nonsense? Since when has it been an act of hostility for women and children to remain quietly in camp, lifting a hand only in the gesture of peace?"

Schmitt reddened angrily. "Mind your tongue!" he snapped. "You are insubordinate."

"Not being in your army, I can't be insubordinate," McGillicuddy snapped. "What has happened speaks for itself."

"Of course you would take such an attitude, being one of them," Schmitt began, when Overton felt compelled to assert his authority.

"Let's have no bickering among ourselves," he implored. "You were over-hasty, Mr. Schmitt. But what's done is done. We have no time to waste."

Neither was appeased. Schmitt saluted, wheeled, and gave the necessary orders. He was a man goaded by ambition, fanatic in his convictions. Clearly he considered himself the victor in both aspects of this skirmish. His salute was carefully precise, but in it was a suggestion of mockery.

Overton noticed, and ordinarily he would not have overlooked it. Schmitt had pushed him into a course of action, though not against his will. Basically their beliefs were the same, and a second in command who was ready to implement them with enthusiasm was an asset, not lightly to be discarded.

That letter of the old chief had shocked him: it

was clearly an official document, promising the protection of the government to a friendly ally. That they should be his slayers, when the Indian had been trying to show them his safeguard, was an irony not lost on Overton, even if Schmitt could shrug it aside.

He was impelled to argue, to explain, to justify himself in the eyes of others, particularly Mike Mc-Chesney. McChesney had read the letter, and what he knew could be extremely damaging if presented before a court of inquiry, or, more particularly, a court-martial. Not that either was within the realm of possibility. And yet the fact remained that Mc-Chesney had knowledge so damning that it might under certain circumstances humiliate or wreck a man.

To explain would be a weakness, but he dismissed that. After all, McChesney was his equal in service, experience and former rank; he was there because Overton had requested his transfer, hoping to profit by his experience. Overton's voice held regret, and it was not necessary to fake that.

"That is the trouble with warfare." He sighed. "Mistakes have a way of occurring, guard against them as one may."

That was true enough. One instance was responsible for the dull ache in McChesney's left arm and shoulder, a pain which grew worse during cold or inclement weather. It was the heritage from a wound inflicted not by the enemy but in a headlong charge in the heat of battle, when other men in blue had swept out suddenly from a fog of smoke, discharging a volley at point-blank range.

Such mistakes occurred, though he could not agree with Overton that any reasonable effort had been made to guard against today's mishap. Nor was there any real regret in Overton for such senseless slaying, as his next words made clear.

"A regrettable error. But no doubt it will have saved them from a lingering and more unpleasant death by cold or starvation. They were shiftless and improvident."

McChesney felt sick at such a wanton massacre. He could not let that pass.

"Some Indians *are* shiftless," he agreed, "but not all. And laziness and poor judgment are not a monopoly of any one race."

"Oh, sure," Overton granted. "Certainly it was too bad that this happened. Believe me, Mr. McChesney, I hold no hate for Indians, as such I know that many people do, having had first-hand experience with atrocities perpetrated against women and children, attacks which often come without warning. As a soldier, I have grown accustomed to warfare. It is never pleasant, but at times it is necessary."

McChesney nodded in silence. Talk would neither undo nor justify a wrong. They had been riding alone, except for Bentley, who jogged a short distance behind. Unconsciously he gripped the saddle-horn with both hands, his face ridged with strain

To Schmitt, there was exhilaration and satisfaction from the clash. To a man of a different nature, it would have been like stripping the bandage from a raw wound.

Overton was warming to his theme.

"I repeat, I have no hate for the red man. My dislike is for the impossible situation in which we all, white and red alike, find ourselves entrapped, as if in a spider's web. Such hate, you might say, is very real, but impersonal. Too many treaties, impossibly foolish contracts, have been made over a span of years with irresponsible and unrepresentative groups. Too much good land has been bargained away."

"Most of the Indians would agree with you." McChesney nodded. "They feel that too much of their land has been lost, leaving them little or nothing in return for the agreements."

"But that's a foolish and short-sighted point of view," Overton protested. "How can footloose nomads make legitimate treaties in the first place, or pretend to grant rights to land which they certainly don't own? Oh, I will grant that in certain instances some have had a reasonable claim. Some in the East and South have shown vestiges of civilization, living in houses, cultivating fields, even enjoying a crude form of government. Perhaps they had something with which to bargain.

"But consider the average tribe, such as the Sioux, Cheyennes or Blackfeet. Along with many others, they claim the same hunting grounds, each disputing the rights of the others. They had no settled habitation, but are footless nomads. It is a travesty to make treaties with such tribes."

"Their claim lies in prior posesssion," McChesney reminded him. "While they may dispute among themselves, they have counted the land as theirs since long before Columbus dubbed red men Indians because he thought he had reached India. Naturally, they regard white men as interlopers."

"A convenient argument, Mr. Chesney, but unjustified by any of the rules of law. To hold land, one must settle and work it, hold it by title and the right of possession."

"Their customs and traditions differ from ours. They don't consider themselves bound by our laws, which they had no part in making."

"A quibble, sir. Mere hunters gain no right of possession merely by the act of passing across territory. Otherwise the gypsies would own half the earth!"

"Your pardon, Major, but is such a claim less justified than that of an explorer who plants a flag and takes possession of vast realms—without settling, founding homes or tilling the soil?"

"There is a distinction. Such claims are backed by the sovereignty of nations—"

"—which are backed by guns—"

"Precisely, sir. Which constitutes a totally different situation. Our mistake as whites has lain in bargaining away too much good land, ground for which we have and will have an ever-increasing need, land *which we must have!* Worse, much of this has been done in haphazard fashion, with boundaries poorly defined, so that such treaties become impossible to keep."

"My understanding, Major, was that our duty as soldiers is to make sure that those treaties are observed by both sides. Whether we like them or not, and how ever good or poor they may be, that is not considered our business."

"I know, and that is the ultimate folly, that those best informed and concerned should have no say in matters of such concern to them. But I repeat, such treaties are impossible to keep. The war is over, the South disrupted. A vast number of once prosperous people have been ruined; the whole country is in ferment. You and I see the consequences. Vast hordes of poor but ambitious people are moving West to find land, to settle and till the soil, to make new beginnings, to civilize a presently savage wasteland. That is a movement which nothing can check or halt—neither governments, edicts, nor hardships, nor the despairing resistance of the scattered tribes who now assert claims to land they never owned."

He could wax almost eloquent. Clearly he believed

passionately in the westward expansion of the nation, which entailed settlement and a constant strengthening of position. And the weight of evidence was on his side.

"I tell you, it's destiny," Overton went on. "The manifest destiny of the nation, of the strong who settled a savage wilderness, pushed across the mountains and on to the Mississippi. But even that did not check them. Already, our flag flies at the Pacific. The land between lies open, even as did that between the great river and the Atlantic. Nothing can halt such a movement. I repeat, sir, to take and to hold is our manifest destiny as a nation and a people."

The argument was familiar to McChesney. Manifest destiny had a challenging ring. It could serve also as a cloak for whatever injustices might be perpetrated in the carrying-out of such a program.

"I've no doubt that you're right," he conceded. "Whether we like it or not, a vast migration is under way. And I'll also grant that neither an edict from Washington nor the army itself can long hold it back."

"Exactly, Mr. McChesney. It is destiny. And as families seek new land, the nomads who once hunted there have to be moved out of the way. Sometimes the methods or the results may be harsh, but it has to be done. When they resist—"

The same fanaticism as had showed in Schmitt's

face burned in his eyes. He was momentarily carried away.

"There is only one answer, one solution. Manifest destiny allows no other. Because these savages insist on fighting us, they will have to be exterminated. Nothing short of that will really solve the problem. So the sooner it is managed, the better for all concerned. This is a practical, a pragmatic matter—in so basic a concept, there is no room for sentiment."

7.

Bentley had continued to ride a short distance behind. He was like a sleepwalker, his eyes open and
going through the motions, but with only a partial
realization of what was happening. The sudden savage assault on the tiny village, the ruthlessness with
which it had been pursued, had shocked him. This
was not warfare as he had pictured it.

Now, without intending to, he had overheard some
of what Overton was saying, and the words slowly
penetrated, piling on top of the rest. As far as they
were concerned, for he was a part of the expedition,
their real objective was not to scout, not even to
police the country split between opposing groups, but
to exterminate an entire race, thereby solving a problem and making room for those who coveted their
land.

Bentley pulled up suddenly and dismounted, stumbling, then was violently sick. Overton looked back,
surprised, his face registering disgust. A soldier was
expected to do his job, not to think.

Jim McGillicuddy rode well ahead, as the duties of a scout required. His mood was as bitter as Bentley's, if less turbulent. His heritage of both Scottish and Indian blood demanded an iron self-control. He had never indulged a bitter humor, as did his father, to speak his feelings with a total contempt for possible consequences.

It would be easy just to keep going, to lose himself so that the army could never trace him; and with any possible consequences to his father removed, the temptation was strong. He would join Running Wolf, one of the chiefs of the Cheyenne and his cousin on his mother's side; join and warn them of the peril inherent in this column of soldiers, who masked sinister intentions by pretending to be on a scout. Afterward, he would fight with his own people.

After what he had witnessed today, that would be easy to do. Though he held Crows in contempt, they too were his people, being red—

He laughed suddenly, the sound short and harsh, and was as abruptly silent. All his days he'd been troubled by his mixed heritage, never quite sure whether he was a white man or an Indian, resentful of being termed a 'breed or mongrel. The mingling of blood of two proud races could scarcely be demeaning—

His brothers had never been bothered by such problems. Whereas he could pass for a white man in appearance, they were Indian both in looks and mentality. They liked and respected their father, but while helping run a ranch, they considered themselves to be Cheyennes, and lately, when trouble had built along the border, they had joined with them to do battle against the whites, should it come to that. In dress, speech attitude and war paint, they would be indistinguishable from all the other warriors.

It had never been so simple for Jim McGillicuddy. Not until today. Now he felt at one with his brothers, with his mother's people. And there was the certainty that his father would approve.

But for the present he might better serve his people by carrying out the duties assigned him as a scout. With nothing to lose and some chance for possible gain, he'd swallow his pride and see what came of it.

Overton gave the order to halt a full hour short of sunset. He did so with reluctance, stifling his impatience. Such wasted time, added delays, could well add up to several extra days before they could get back to Lookout. He had undertaken this expedition with a mixture of eagerness and reluctance; eagerness because he had always been a man of action, a fighting soldier rather than a planner or desk man. Routine had tied him too long to a desk, to a horizon bounded by the limits of a stockade and parade ground.

Actually, he had sniffed the battle from afar. There would be clashes, battle, the acrid fragrance of gun-smoke to tickle the nostrils. Blood.

Once a weasel had tasted the red tide, its appetite became insatiable. Overton did not admit even to himself that a man might harbor such a craving, but the excitement had blown at him like a wind, strong, compelling.

Clashes, even skirmishes, could perhaps—even probably—be avoided. But he'd known, without conscious recognition, that they would not be.

At the same time, he'd measured carefully the expected time of the arrival at the fort of Maggie Trout. It would be not only discourteous but distressing not to be there to welcome her upon her arrival.

A different quality of excitement, as strong as the excitement at the prospect of battle and equally pleasing, had been kindled in him at his first sight of her. Better acquaintance, an exchange of letters and the tug of memory had enhanced the picture which he carried in his mind. Margaret Trout would always be a woman to come home to, and lucky the man for whom she waited.

He had made his calculations as carefully as possible and had decided that both prospects were feasible. Duty, he had persuaded himself, was impelling. With so much unrest among the tribes, he should command this expedition, not trusting so considerable a force to a lesser officer.

That had represented a change of mind. His original plan had been for Mike McChesney to lead. Not only was McChesney experienced, but his knowledge of Indians exceeded Overton's.

The trouble had been that, once McChesney arrived, a wide gap in their philosophies had become apparent. Overton had decided to please himself.

Captain Schmitt had been an alternate possibility. He was a fighting man, a soldier who shared Overton's philosophy of battle as well as his hatred for Indians.

That was the trouble. Headlong hate was destructive. Schmitt had never learned to control his hostility to Indians, and he declined to try.

Overton ordered an early stop where cottonwoods lifted at the curve of a small creek. The grove insured wood for the cook fires, the convenience of water. Still better, the land lay wide and open, protection against ambush or surprise.

McChesney's horse planted its feet in easy flowing water which washed above the fetlocks. It dipped its nose and drank thirstily, then held its lips in the water. McChesney allowed it to dawdle. It had earned the right.

Flags waved green beside a mud bank, where the ripple widened to a long pool. The faint splash of a waterfall, hidden by the bend, was both musical and a revelation. Long tracks in the mud, the white gleam of a willow stump, completed the story. Beaver had barricaded the creek, holding back the current, making a pool and a waterfall.

A muskrat swam at the edge of the shadows, its brown head cleaving the water, its beady eyes regarding him watchfully. It was gone with a small splash as Mike pulled his pony into motion.

He was not surprised, in the closing softness of dusk, to be joined by Bentley and two other lieutenants as he strolled along the far bank. Next to the close proximity of a fort's compound, there was no quicker way to get to know one's fellows than on such a ride, where danger could lurk behind every clump of brush or dip of land, where a man's philosophy of life and death showed for what it was, even if no word was spoken, no overt sign made.

George Beasley was a ramrod type of man, both in temperament and build, intense, eager, yet repressed. Bill Zimmerman was his opposite in most respects, short, comfortably fleshed, his grin frank and engaging. They had seen long service together.

In the aftermath of the slaughter he had caught strong disapproval in Beasley's eyes, and a shock in Zimmerman's almost matching Bentley's. Soldiers and officers, they had accepted the inevitable, being unable to change it. But sickness of the soul as well as of the flesh left its mark.

There was nothing unusual in the fact that a trio of officers should stroll for exercise, chatting companionably in an idle hour. Nor did McChesney find it odd for them to join him. Each recognized the mutuality of their viewpoints. It was a drawing together as though for protection; they were a tiny minority in the larger group which saw nothing wrong in the events of the day.

They paused, watching the dark waters of the pool. A rising moon cast an uncertain light, seeming to falter as it swam in troubled depths. The smell of horse sweat and saddle leather was replaced by the muskiness of beaver, the pungency of water grasses in a smaller pool below the dam.

Bentley burst out suddenly. The words, like his outrage, had been long repressed. Now they came explosively.

"It was murder, sheer murder, any way you look at it!"

A beaver, ghostly in the far shadows, slapped the water with a sound like a pistol shot. Ripples ran the length of the pool. Zimmerman nodded, his broad easy face tight.

"The thing was a massacre," he confirmed. "Uncalled for—without justification."

Beasley echoed them passionately.

"I hold no brief for Indians, as a class or a tribe," he said. "I've seen some of their work, and it turned me sick. But after watching atrocities by men of my own race, trained and supposedly disciplined, considered civilized—"

He allowed the words to hang in the air. As if by common consent, all three looked to McChesney, standing silent, his glance still ranging the now untroubled waters. The drip and splash of the spill reminded him of a sleigh ride, of the silver bells worn by the horses.

"It *was* murder," Bentley repeated stubbornly, "Women, children—and that poor old devil of a brave! He wasn't trying to fight back, only to make a gesture of friendship. No fair-minded man could mistake it for anything else."

". bad, sad business." Beasley sighed. "To fight a battle is one thing. I've been in enough to know the difference. Most times I was scared half to death, and at best it's a chancy, unpleasant business. But when it's in the open, man to man—well, I suppose it has to be done. But this other—paugh!"

"What do you think, Mr. McChesney?" Bentley demanded. "I could see by your face that you disapproved as strongly as we did. But you've had more experience. What can we do?"

"Now there's the rub," McChesney returned soberly. "I'll agree that I liked what happened no better than the rest of you. But as Mr. Beasley points out, war is an unpleasant business at best, yet it happens to be a soldier's job. And we're soldiers."

"But a soldier has a code of honor! I've always thought of myself in terms of that code, striving to remember that an officer is a gentleman." Zimmerman's tone was harsh with protest.

"There was nothing gentlemanly about today's business," Bentley growled.

They were asking for advice, for help, and McChesney could not put them off with platitudes.

"I wish I could give you a fair and sure answer, gentlemen. I can't. I share your views in regard to what happened today, also finding no justification or excuse. But that was not the first time that such a thing has happened, and almost certainly it will not be the last. Other men hold equally strong yet opposite convictions, often, I must grant, with good cause.

"I feel that such a policy—and I am sure it was done by policy, not impulse—as was followed by Captain Schmitt is wrong. But we serve the government of the United States; we are officers of the army. All that I can say is, as long as we remain such, we must keep in mind that soldiers obey orders. In the long run, that is essential to government as opposed to chaos, to law and order as contrasted with— oh, what's the use? Good night, gentlemen."

8.

"The major wants to see you—now!"

McChesney had one boot off and was tugging at the other, his mind feeling as bruised and swollen as his feet. And with better cause, he thought, though the boots had been sweaty, the leather over-tight.

His head jerked up at the bark of triumph in O'Reilly's voice, a malicious overtone which he made no effort to conceal. Having delivered his message, the sergeant turned about, neglecting to salute.

McChesney let him go. Such thinly veiled disrespect amounted almost to insubordination, but he was past caring. Once this journey was accomplished, he'd be through with army life, and regulations and discipline seemed trivial, seemed no longer to matter.

He would need but a single guess as to why he was being summoned at that hour, immediately after the four of them had returned. Someone had spied from the darkness, eavesdropping on Beasley, Zimmerman, Bentley and himself, and had run to carry tales with the maliciousness of a small boy. Nor did he require a second guess as to who that might be.

Overton, unlike the rest, rated a tent. He was standing in front of it as McChesney approached, feet wide-planted before a freshly fed blaze, the reddish hues of the firelight matching the angry ruddiness of cheeks and jowls. Captain Schmitt loomed at one side, shadowy yet solid. In the gloom, McChesney could feel his heavy regard. It held the quality of a puma stretched along a limb, waiting to launch itself upon its prey in the trail below.

Lieutenant Bentley was the next to arrive, breathless with haste, flustered by his emotions. He drew up suddenly at the sight of Schmitt and McChesney, and his rigidity showed understanding and a mounting anger.

A screech owl chose that moment to gibber from the high shadows of the looming trees. Curiously, it was Schmitt who started at that hellish mockery, as though finding it directed at himself.

Beasley and Zimmerman came together, faintly apprehensive for all the correctness of their attitude, Sergeant O'Reilly lurked in the background. The major's gaze roved darkly.

"I doubt that any of you require an explanation as to why you have been summoned here, so hard upon the heels of the impromptu conference which you chose to hold and which was overheard by Captain Schmitt. He considered the attitude of so many officers as being not merely reprehensible but as threatening the welfare of the expedition. And I cannot but concur.

"You have the right to your own opinions, of course, but there are times when such views should be kept to oneself. It is not the business of the army to make policy, merely to execute it. That applies even more to officers. To follow a misguided path is to stumble into a thicket. In the service such a course—or slipping away to hold secret conferences— is especially dangerous."

He paused for a dragging moment, then added heavily:

"Mr. McChesney gave you good advice: that, as soldiers, you should obey orders. I can do no better than emphasize what he said. But I must caution you, for your own good and the welfare of the service, to guard your tongues. Words—such words as murder —are strong, even in a man's thoughts. Let there be an end to that sort of thing."

He dismissed them with no personal reprimands, as though uncertain in his own mind as to the wisdom of what he had done. Tugging anew at his boots, McChesney reflected on the man with a wry amazement. Overton was torn by a conflict between mixed emotions and desires, a man unsure of himself and so inclined to ruthlessness when forced to action. Having felt compelled to explain himself, which was a form of excuse, to summon them at the complaint of a man who admittedly had been spying—too late he had recognized his folly and been unable to draw back.

McChesney could almost pity the man. The trouble was that weakness and ruthlessness fed upon each other, and the consequences were not pleasant to think about.

The night brought change. As though making the most of the hours of darkness, the sun and salubrious temperatures had drawn back, and a gray haze of cloud was mixed with a wind which hinted at the vast sweep of untrammeled plain across which it might soon push with blizzard force. The hunters, absent from tepees and reservation, would be warned and impelled to haste, to greater efforts while there was yet time, just as the beavers, gnawing furiously at bush and tree, would sink their cuttings to pond bottom against the need of tasty morsels in the Moon of the Long Cold.

Newly awakened, the men were red-eyed, stiff-jointed from the accumulated fatigue of the trail and the change in weather. They took out their frustration by swearing at their horses, eying one another and their officers with a veiled distrust. They had been asleep during that brief meeting of the night and were only now stirring, yet somehow the knowledge had spread, and they were as wary as a stag venturing to a pool to drink. McChesney had seen that before; it was something to be explained, but it happened. Troopers would still obey, but ingrained wrongness was like the stiffness in muscles which neither the heat of the sun nor the push of exercise could drive out.

Rigid politeness, a precise correctness, marked each officer. If he had not quite understood before, Overton knew now: something had been lost, a new and different quality added.

Jim McGillicuddy had missed all that. He had slipped away from camp in the early darkness, scouting ahead. The sun, however veiled, was high when he rejoined them, appearing suddenly out of a draw, materializing like a ghost from a great emptiness. Men who had scanned the vastness of the prairie, nervously reassuring themselves that it could conceal nothing, swore in disbelief. Some remembered that the scout, though a Scotsman, was also Indian, and eyed the land with mounting unease.

Overton had ridden by himself all through the forenoon. His inclination to garrulity, to sociability, seemed suddenly lost. His eyes were remote and hooded, but he lifted a gauntleted hand in a gesture for his officers to gather as the scout prepared to report.

"I approached the Cheyenne camp near the base of Two Buttes," McGillicuddy said carefully. His face looked strained and drawn with a private apprehension. He was anxious to make his point, remembering the women at the large camp as well as at the small, the old men, the children. He elaborated.

"It is a hunting camp, in no sense a war expedition. Apparently the hunting has been good. The women, the children, even the old men and aged squaws are furiously busy curing the meat which has been brought in, adding berries, making pemmican, all manner of food to be stored against the needs of winter. Even papooses watch bright-eyed and without complaint." He swept a hand toward the leaden sky, the wailing rise of the wind. "They smell the winter."

With an Indian, any red man, the argument would have been potent. War parties did not travel with their women, their children and the old. And when winter was imminent, their thought was of food, of skins for blankets and warm tepees, of shelter and survival. Summer was the season for war, after winter snows vanished under blazing suns, and blood, like streams, ran riotously. But when the grizzly sought his den and the groundhog its burrow, nature drew close and the pulse slowed for the time of sleep.

The trouble was that most white men did not understand. Between the minds was a fundamental difference, an unbridgeable gap. What was simple and clear to one was beyond the other's grasp. McChesney could read it in the faces about him. McGillicuddy had made his point, but it had passed like a high arrow.

"How many braves?" Overton queried, and for

him that was the heart of the matter.

McGillicuddy answered as honestly as he could.

"Between four and five hundred, I would estimate."

That meant the bulk of the Cheyenne nation, a formidable force. Schmitt exchanged glances with Overton. Braves were warriors. Women and children did not count.

"In this Cheyenne camp?" Overton persisted.

"Yes." McGillicuddy was part white, and he sensed something and did not like it. "But they are all hunters—"

"And ready to take any sort of game they come across, I wouldn't doubt," Schmitt cut in. "It's a devil of a big party to be *off* the reservation, Major."

"And their allies—are there other Indians besides the Cheyennes?" Overton was persistent.

"Yes. There's another camp perhaps a mile away. Arapahoes, also curing meat as fast as possible."

"With how many braves?"

"Perhaps—" McGillicuddy paused and amended the world proudly— "probably a couple of hundred."

He was sensing the changed atmosphere, the tension which had flowered overnight. From the initial clash the situation had somehow altered into a contest for leadership, regardless of rank, for supremacy. Too late, Overton had realized where he had erred in allowing Schmitt to influence him, to tell him what to do and how to act. Schmitt still prodded, and

Overton was intent on showing himself as not only
the commander but also on demonstrating an equal
ruthlessness when the circumstances demanded

"Did you go into the camp?" he asked.

Jim nodded. "Certainly. I wished to make sure."

"Sure?" Schmitt's tone was ironic. "Of what?"

"Of their real intentions." McGillicuddy could
mock in turn. "Red men can be as hypocritical as
whites when it suits their purpose. At this camp,
Running Wolf is chief, and he gave me his firm
pledge that, as soon as the meat is dried and ready
for the packs, they will return to their winter quarters on the reservation. They are overlooking certain
provocations—"

He left it at that, and only McChesney could
guess how earnestly he must have argued, pointing
out that for the common good, recent outrages should
be overlooked. It would have cost the scout an effort
to adopt such a line, which was contrary to his inclinations. But an Indian was first and last a prag-
matist. He could fight savagely in battle, then with-
draw from the struggle to save lives and avoid defeat, and feel no stigma of cowardice. Retreat at such
a time was merely showing good sense.

In this situation it was the same. Winter, with the
threat of starvation, was on the march. Conditions
could become ten times worse should this uneasy
column in blue run wild.

"Provocations?" Schmitt repeated. "Are *you* ac-

cusing us of creating provocations, McGillicuddy—
for having carried out our orders?"

He was a firebrand, this Schmitt, white-hot beneath an icy exterior. But that the goading words
were aimed at Overton rather than the scout, Jim
McGillicuddy could hardly know.

His face flamed in turn, but he swiftly brought
his temper under control. They might call him mongrel and half-breed, but in that moment he was the
master.

"There have been provocations on both sides, Captain. For his part, Chief Running Wolf is doing his
best to keep his people under control, because his
desire for peace is genuine."

"That wasn't what I asked you, McGillicuddy.
I—"

Overton's anger flared. He understood, if McGillicuddy did not.

"*I* am asking the questions, Captain!" A small devil
seemed to creep into his eyes and voice. "This Chief
Running Wolf—do you vouch for him?"

"I do, sir. Completely."

"Then you know him well? You are—perhaps—
related to him in some way?"

McGillicuddy colored again, but remained grave.
"He is my cousin."

"Indeed! And a firm friend of the white men!"

McGillicuddy had restrained his temper admira-
bly. But he was white as well as red, with his father's

peppery nature. There were limits to even an iron control.

"As firm as Chief Little Wolf."

Little Wolf, in a dying gesture, had brandished a document from the government, attesting to his friendship and loyalty. The example was not lost on Overton.

"Do you have any suggestions?"

"Since you ask, yes. I do not believe that there is any need to go further, sir. I am sure that the over-all situation is favorable to an uneventful winter."

"A winter of resting and feasting, to prepare for a bloody outbreak once the weather warms, eh?" Overton's voice was soft. "I asked for suggestions, not advice. Your business is to guide and scout. *I* make the decisions."

His voice held a sudden rasp.

"Forward!"

9.

Mike rode somberly, aloof if not alone. He was violating his own rule, he realized, the only rule by which a soldier could live: to take one day at a time, not reaching out, rarely thinking beyond the moment and its duty. Those who allowed their imagination to push too far reaped trouble and frustration.

But that letter from his sister had opened new vistas, expanded still further by Major Overton's confidence that he too expected feminine company at the fort. Visitors of such quality were almost as rare as the infrequent flashing of a celestial comet across the dark of wintry skies.

Conditions being as they were, with a sudden tightness running through the ranks, it was a relief to dwell on such a diversion. For the rest, he would follow the rule, closing his mind to a situation which he was powerless to alter.

The trouble with such a resolution lay in keeping it. Others were having the same difficulty. Opinions, convictions lightly held at the outset, were solidifying, altering as subtly as snow. Softly falling, it could be intangible as cotton; then, after freezing and crusting, it underwent vastly more of a change than was apparent, hardening to an implacable pattern which would break before it would bend.

Showdown loomed ahead, and it would not be long in coming. Overton's rejection of Jim's suggestion, his order to go on, had made it all but inevitable. They were nearing the big camps of the Indians, with the buttes looming against the horizon.

A reunion at Fort Lookout would be a fitting climax to such a ride—but only if a clash could be avoided.

Overton prided himself that the decision belonged to him, according to whatever orders he chose to issue. But he deluded himself.

These men were keyed to slaughter, led by men between whom a fatal rivalry was building. There was no glory in a wide-ranging scout, however risky the ride. But a savage clash, a sweeping victory, was a way—the only way under existing circumstances—to preferment and promotion.

They might have turned back, as Jim McGillicuddy had urged. That had been the time of choice. Overton, prodded by Schmitt, had chosen to go on.

The ground fell away toward a distant line of willows. Grass which had greened with spring now cured and brown, rustled silkily under the hoofs of horses. Grasshoppers stirred sluggishly before the invasion. Insects mustered small clouds and hung tantalizingly before eyes and faces. Birds, which had flocked by scores and hundreds when the expedition had set out from Lookout, had vanished like a secret harbinger of storm. No sun flashed silver from the creek. Gullies crouched behind upthrusts of brush, roughening the landscape.

Something stirred, like a creature scuttling for cover. Private Rance Beauvois, riding ahead and to the right called an excited warning.

"Something off there — might have been an Indian —"

His words carried far and clear. Men jerked to attention as though pulled by a common string. *Skulkers* —

Luck favored Captain Schmitt. Major Overton chanced to be riding near the rear of the column. Schmitt was out front. Always a chance taker. he had modeled his career according to a simple principle. A bold man forced the play, and if he won his gamble, there was never much criticism for success. Only failures drew reprimands.

"There are several, certainly more than one, hiding in the brush," Schmitt announced and a trace of excitement made the words slap. "An ambush, perhaps —"

Lieutenant Bentley rode at his side. Bentley was staring also, breathing hard. Schmitt felt a rising contempt for the tenderfoot. *A man could be too damned careful—*

"Form a line," he instructed O'Reilly. "Prepare for action."

The rifles were lifting when Bentley gasped a startled discovery.

"Hold your fire! They're whites!"

So it proved as, moments later, they came out from the gulch, struggling into full view, plainly catching their first glimpse of the line of blue riders drawn up and regarding them so suspiciously. Schmitt's breath expelled in a gust of relief. That had been a near thing—the senseless fools should have known better! Who, by the wildest stretch of imagination, would have looked for whites at such a place and time?

Yet whites they unquestionably were. The illusion that they might be Indians was fostered by every appearance short of the color of their skin. A single brownish-gray horse, each rib of which was clearly visible, drew a travois—an Indian rig of saplings fastened into a sort of sleigh, on which goods could be piled and a squaw or child or old man might ride. It was the only vehicle developed and horse-drawn by these children of the plains, but practical and useful when a move was made from one camp to another.

This travois was almost certainly of Indian manufacture, not an imitation hastily put together by unskilled workers. It was piled with as many goods as it could conveniently carry or the weary cayuse could drag.

A woman led the horse, looking not unlike a squaw. A man rode, not too comfortably, watched over and aided somewhat by a half-grown girl. Viewed in the open, the procession was meager, smaller than excited imaginings had pictured it when it had been glimpsed through a covering of trees and brush.

Overton galloped up, staring. His glance raked angrily as he assessed the preparations which Schmitt had made, and how nearly they had come to being carried out. But he made no comment, offered no reprimand. He had instructed Schmitt to be on the alert, each of them knowing precisely what that order implied.

He was aghast at how close to a mistake they had come, and even Schmitt looked shaken. Three people, whites, down on their luck, wandering through the heart of a wilderness aswarm with Indians—even the evidence of their eyes made it no more believable.

The forlorn expedition had halted, the washboard-ribbed cayuse turning eagerly to crop the grass. The woman stared incredulously, her face working, on the verge of tears. The man alone of the trio seemed cheerful, almost eager.

"Knew our luck had turned, an' for the better," he

proclaimed. " 'Mandy grew a mite discouraged when I broke my leg, and was worse let down when our team straddled a coiled rattler right under their feet and kicked the smithereens out of our old wagon. Then one horse was snake-bit and swole up so it had to be kilt. Looked bad, for a fact, but like I told her, no matter how dark the night, there's always a fresh new day to follow. And when those Indians come along, Mandy was feared they'd take our scalps, 'stead of which they took pity on us and fixed us up with this travelin' rig, and give us food and a robe or so for warmth. I knew right then our luck 'd changed and was bound to keep on gettin' better."

That was essentially his story. They had set out for the West months and miles before, joining up with a wagon train, somehow making it beyond the expectations of more reasonable beings. When sickness and ill luck had decimated the train, and they had lost the others, as well as themselves, Larkin Leaman had refused to be discouraged, but his wife, more realistic, had perceived how nearly hopeless was their plight.

McChesney, listening sympathized with her. An indomitable spirit was a necessary asset for those who set out pioneering, but good sense and sound judgment were equally vital, and Leaman, it was apparent, was a visionary and a dreamer, hopelessly cheerful and completely impractical. There was a saying in the country that the Lord looked out for fools and tenderfeet, and in this instance that seemed to be borne out.

It had been their good fortune, at the nadir of trouble, to be found by Indians who pitied them and had gone out of their way to help. Others might have reacted quite differently.

The covering brush and coulee through which they struggled had created a distorted picture, an unexpected hazard. Overton, conscious of how great that risk had been, was doing all in his power to make amends. The march was temporarily halted. Dr. Kirby, who rode as tirelessly as any man of the regiment, a gray badger of a man, examined the broken limb and pronounced Mrs. Leaman's handiwork to be good.

"The bone is properly set, splinted, and however painful the rigors of travel, it is well on the way to healing," he said. "Few could have done so well. I salute you, ma'am."

Amanda Leaman's faded cheeks colored with pleasure. Compliments were frugal fare in that land.

"She ain't done bad." Larkin admitted. "Was inclined to get weepy and lose her head, but I kept mine, and told her what to do at each step. The Lord watches over His own, I always say."

To continue their journey would be risky, though no more than before. Of late they had been traveling almost aimlessly, Mrs. Leaman fearful of the coming winter, struggling on determinedly but without much hope. Now they could be pointed toward the fort, and Major Overton, still uncomfortably picturing in his mind's eye what might have happened, outfitted them with three additional horses, gentle enough for each to ride on, the decrepit nag able to pack such supplies as could not be tied behind saddles. Larkin could ride with scarcely more discomfort than on the dragging, jolting travois.

He brushed aside the man's fulsome thanks, explaining that the horses were a loan, not a gift. After they reached the fort, final disposition could be made. As a destination, it was far enough in the future.

"*If* they reach it," Schmitt agreed speaking to Sergeant O'Reilly. "Mounted on such horses, they'll be more of a temptation to wandering redskins than before."

"But we'll be between them and the main bunch," O'Reilly pointed out.

"True. And I hope they make it, for the sake of the child and her mother," Schmitt conceded, then went on to express his amazement. He had discovered in Seamus O'Reilly a kindred spirit, in whom it was safe to confide.

"Beats me how the major carries on," he added. "Of course if an accident had happened, it would have been too bad, though it might have solved their problems for them. For I can foresee nothing else ahead for them. Otherwise, what real difference would it have made? Overton would say of Indians that it was good riddance. But because these are white—"

He was silent a minute, then finished the thought.

"Where I came from, they'd be described as trash—white trash, looked down on even by honest niggers. So what's the difference?"

Seamus O'Reilly shook his head.

"The captain is a realist," he said, "a realist and a soldier. But the major is not a hypocrite, whatever else he may be. His skin is white, and it denotes a proud race. Black or yellow, red or brown—to him all such are inferior, scarcely human." The sergeant gave a twist to his mustache. A realist, he was also a cynic.

"Such a belief makes it easier to be a good soldier; makes it as easy to kill an Indian as to shoot a buffalo, that its tongue may be a feast at supper, while the wolves dine well on all the rest."

10.

Snow came spitting out of an angry sky, small, harsh flakes, buffeted by a twisting wind. Such a storm was unseasonable, and it did not last long, giving way to a cold rain. But it seemed a portent, a warning that the winter to come might be as much a test for survival as the hunters feared. For the old men, who dreamed in the sun or crouched above the fires, and the ancient women on whom had fallen the toil and blight had read the signs even in the heat of midsummer and croaked their prophecies.

Heeding them, the tribes had bestirred themselves. There was a risk in setting forth after game, since the good hunting grounds lay beyond the boundaries of the reservations. Somehow the fat lands which their forefathers had cherished had been whittled away, not always by treaty. To stray again would be chancy, but to starve would mean only a slower doom.

Jim McGillicuddy pondered as he rode, shivering

in the sudden cold. Briefly his ears had burned with
rage, overhearing an order by Captain Schmitt addressed to Seamus O'Reilly.

"Watch him, Sergeant. And if he should attempt
to take off, to sneak away and warn the enemy—
kill him."

His anger had been succeeded by the reflection
that there was no need for him to carry a warning,
since the riders in blue were under constant observation.

What worried the scout was his inability to per-
suade the major that it was actually a hunting expedition, and only that. A good officer weighed carefully the reports of his scouts. Here the key lay
in the term used by Schmitt—the enemy. Portents
of trouble were as easy to read as the flaring of sun-
dogs in a winter sky.

Lieutenant Bentley was similarly troubled. He felt
that he was learning fast, but his trouble was that
he could not shut his mind to what he saw, leaving
the responsibility to his superiors. As a soldier, that
was his duty. But as a man—

Many times he had been reminded that he was
an officer and a gentleman, and those terms carried
obligations. He was sticking his neck out, but that
was a part of duty. He swung his horse along the
major's, saluting.

"I request permission to speak, Major: to discuss

certain matters, if I may."

Overton regarded him warily. He could guess what was in the lieutenant's mind, and he was half-inclined to reprimand him with a curt refusal. But Bentley was earnest as well as young, and he nodded.

"Of course, Mr. Bentley. Is something troubling you?"

"In a way, sir, yes." Bentley's troubled breath was a long sigh. "I've been thinking about the Leamans, whom you befriended so generously; and of how the Indians also were good to them, when they might so easily have—well, have killed them. It seems to me to confirm other reports that the Indians have strayed from the reservation only to hunt, and are behaving peacefully, demonstrating their good will."

"A piece of luck for the Leamans," Overton grunted.

"Yes sir. But Mr. McGillicuddy is of the opinion that they will return peacefully to their lodges, of their own accord, once they have secured meat."

Overton's face was impassive. But he'd gotten himself into this by allowing others to argue and discuss—all because he felt impelled to justify his own course. And after all, what did it matter whether one went by the book or overstepped a bit? The best officers were likely to be sloppy disciplinarians, but the finest he'd ever known had been an awesome fighting man in action, whose men were ready to follow him to hell and back, almost literally, if called upon to do so.

"There is something to what you say," he granted. "And I appreciate the spirit in which you bring this up, Mr. Bentley. But consider the situation. We are out on scout, with a large force, while at the same time, a disturbingly large number of hostiles are off the reservation. If we fail even to approach them, to make a show of strength, they might misunderstand."

"I suppose that is possible."

"Not only possible, but I would feel that I was derelict in my duty if I turned aside at this point. We are faced with an increasingly touchy situation, one which worsens with the passage of time. Only by respect, and respect in such a situation is born of fear, are we going to keep the lid on, keep the situation under control."

It sounded plausible, and Bentley credited him with believing what he said. But he was unconvinced.

"That's my point exactly, sir—to keep the lid on, to avoid an outbreak, from whatever cause. But it appeared to me that we were dangerously close to firing upon the Leamans, while they were merely glimpsed through the brush and while everyone supposed them to be red men rather than white. As was the case with that earlier encampment, where women and children were killed—"

He paused, realizing that he had been on the

verge of using the word murder, a virtual accusation. Overton was being patient with him, and he must not overstep reasonable bounds.

"What I'm trying to say, sir, is that Mr. McGillicuddy knows these people, and in his opinion—"

Overton's patience was dangerously strained. Bentley's words amounted to a charge that he had been guilty of a murderous outrage, which he feared would be repeated. The phrases were polite, but this was insufferable.

"Mr. McGillicuddy's opinion, you say? But you are forgetting one thing, Lieutenant. The name is white and Scotch—but the man is an Indian!"

Bentley blinked in bewilderment.

"But he is a scout. And my understanding was that most scouts are Indians—"

"Quite so. And because of that they are efficient and useful, up to a point. But when you are faced with the responsibilities of command, Mr. Bentley, you must keep in mind that an Indian will naturally favor his own people."

"But Mr. McGillicuddy is half-white—"

"He's neither fish nor fowl!" Overton's contempt was undisguised. "He's a mongrel, the son of a squaw. It is from such mixtures that traitors are spawned."

Bentley went white. It would be better to thank his superior for listening to him and to terminate the discussion as quickly as possible. But there was a stubborn streak in Bentley, a rashness which drove him even as a similar trait worked in Overton.

"But surely, sir, a distinction must be made for individuals, regardless of their possible ancestry or color—"

"I can't go along with such a notion," Overton pronounced. "A trace of dye in a bucket of water can stain the whole, just as a drop of poison in a glass of water can be fatal. A mongrel's a mongrel."

His tone was as argumentative as it was challenging. The white in Bentley's cheeks had been replaced by red.

"If I may be permitted to cite an example, sir—more or less from my own experience; one which I find painful, but impelling—"

"Oh, go on," Overton grunted.

"My grandfather was a plantation owner, and he kept many slaves. He treated them well, by prevailing standards, but he had been born and bred a New Englander, and he had a Puritan conscience, along rather rigid lines. He took strong issue with the local parson, who encouraged Negroes to attend church, the young ones to study in Sunday school. My grandfather insisted that such behavior was sheer hypocrisy, to befuddle the minds of the blacks with an impossible hope for the hereafter, merely so that they would be better behaved in their present condition. Lacking a soul, they could not enter into an eternity of paradise. If he believed them creatures with souls, he could not justify buying and selling them as cattle, holding them enslaved."

"He set a problem for himself," Overton granted, interested.

"He was a strict man, according to his own standards. These became an impossible burden when he discovered that a slave about his own age, of whom he was as fond as he permitted himself to be of a black, was his own brother. If a colored man possessed no soul—*where did he draw the line!*"

Overton drew a deep breath. Bentley, he realized belatedly, was overly clever at debate.

"And the sequel to this tale?"

"My grandfather died of a stroke, which perhaps was the kindest way out."

Overton regarded his companion somewhat askance. His shrug was elaborate.

"You are trying to tell me, sir, that blood or color of skin makes no difference. I cannot agree. I am of the same school as your ancestor. If you are familiar with Scripture, you may recall that the black man was cursed for his sin and doomed forever to be a member of an inferior and enslaved race. Red or black, I see no difference."

"Am I to understand, sir, that you find nothing wrong in killing Indians because they are Indians?"

"You are over-bold, Mr. Bentley—but I admire

courage in a soldier. And I'll answer you as straight
forwardly. I find it regrettable, but necessary. It is
manifest destiny that the white man, having settled
these shores, should tame the wilderness and found
in its place a new and greater nation—one more magnificent than anything the world has hitherto known;
a land of opportunity for all—even for such misfits
as the Leamans."

"For all? But you mean only for whites. What
you are virtually saying, sir, is that the Indians must
be exterminated to make room for the whites."

"I regret the necessity, but that is a fair statement
of the situation. To take and subdue the land is our
manifest destiny as a people and as a nation. There
is no room for two cultures—if we go so far as to suppose that the Indians' deserves such a term—one cul-
ture highly civilized, the other inherently savage.
No, there is no room for savages or for a mongrel
race. Under the circumstances, only one solution is
possible."

Despite what he had seen and heard, such bluntness took Bentley by surprise. Major Overton had the
façade of a cultured gentleman, but at heart he was
a fanatic, and, carried away, he had betrayed his
true conviction. It explained what had happened,
and, far more frightening, was a portent of the future.

"Extermination? You are saying that the only good
Indian is a dead Indian?"

"Others have perceived that long before I grasped it. To some, such a course, such necessity, may seem heartless, even brutal. But the swift stroke of a knife is in the end far less painful than a drawn-out endless ordeal."

"But what about the treaties which have been made? What about the guarantees that have been given, ever since the Pilgrims set foot on Plymouth Rock? Many, if not most of these, have been entered into by our own government—"

Overton brushed that aside with a sweeping gesture.

"Some of those were dictated by expediency, but many were the act of fools. In any case, they are merely obstacles in the path of the white man, barriers holding back the march of progress. Even if we really wanted to, and used all the force of the entire army—*and augmented it by ten times the present force*—it would be impossible to stay the onsweeping tide of homeseekers, of emigrants from east of the Big River; not to mention those from beyond the seas.

"They have beheld a vision, they have dreamed a dream, they have come seeking land, and land they will have! Shall the government, through its army, slay its own citizens to protect lesser and savage races? Decidedly not. Since one or the other must stand aside, it is surely better that the few, the ignorant, the lesser, should go. And the sooner that is accomplished, the more merciful the end result, the less blood of the innocent will be needlessly spilled!"

Abruptly he wheeled his horse and galloped away, terminating the discussion. Bentley watched him go, appalled. The worst of it was that Overton was completely sincere, convinced that the end justified the means.

Two Buttes were looming against the skyline suddenly, ominously close. Somewhere in the vicinity was the camp of the Cheyennes. With a foreboding of despair, Bentley shook his head.

11.

Uneasiness was like a muddy tributary spilling into a clear stream in Overton's mind. He glanced around apprehensively, though of course there was nothing to see. Officers or men were careful to hold to an unwritten but prescribed distance at such a time, to keep their faces carefully blank. But he had raised his voice in a burst of excitement, and sounds sometimes had unexpected carrying power.

Temper boiled higher, as in a kettle too closely covered. What right did these others have to judge, to form opinions about him? Certainly he did not enjoy the business of killing, whether it was Indians or otherwise; not the way some others did. To them it was almost a form of sport. With him it was an unpleasant duty.

Since it was necessary, nothing should turn him from that, certainly not the claptrap of specious arguments. He decided that he'd been overly indulgent, allowing protest to get out of bounds. But he'd been anxious to convince everyone of his sincerity.

Especially himself. But that was something he dared not admit, least of all to himself.

He beckoned to O'Reilly, giving a curt instruction. "Send McGillicuddy to me."

The scout's face was faintly inquiring as he responded, but he asked no questions.

"It occurred to me that it might be better all around if you were to ride ahead and warn the Indian camp of our approach," Overton explained. "We certainly don't intend our arrival to come as a surprise, or anything of that nature."

It sounded like a reassuring gesture, but McGillicuddy did not accept it as such. The very wording denoted a conflict if not confusion in Overton's mind. It was, Jim decided, the highland blood in him, the long heritage of suspicion, particularly as regarded foes who came with a gift in one hand and a gun in the other. Or it might be a sharpening of such traits in the mixed blood which ran in his veins.

Neither Running Wolf nor his brothers were at the camp when he arrived. Along with nearly all the other able-bodied men, they were still out, busy bringing in meat from a recent lucky hunt. They had found buffalo, and that was a rarity.

The women, the children and the elderly were busy. A single chief, Old Beaver, remained, and

McGillicuddy reported what Overton had said.

"But I don't trust him," he added bluntly. "I have seen a wolf trotting playfully at the edge of a bunch of cattle, rolling in the dirt where they have lain, gradually mingling with them until they become so accustomed to him that they pay no attention. Then, all at once, a stray calf is set upon, and the wolf is a wolf."

"I thank our brother for the warning," Old Beaver said. "But we have nothing to worry about. Anyone can see that this is a hunter's camp, a peaceful village. Besides, I have a flag such as the soldiers carry, with the same stripes and stars. It was given to me as a token of enduring firendship when I visited the city of the Great White Father. When it is unfurled, those who stand beneath it are assured of its protection."

"Just the same, I think that you should send word to those who are in the field, warning them of the approach of armed men," Jim insisted.

"I have no one to send," Old Beaver pointed out. "As you can see, we are all very busy."

Jim said no more. Argument was a waste of breath, and there was no time to lose. He went on by himself, his chief regret that no fresh pony was available.

It was Old Beaver's confidence in the potency of the many-starred flag, the assurance so solemnly given him many moons before that, as a proven friend of the white man, he and his people would be safe, which led to their undoing. True to McGillicuddy's report, the chief looked up to see a long file of mounted men approaching, and for a moment, despite his confidence in the cleanness of his own heart, he was disturbed, remembering Jim's word. For Jim, after all, was not merely a white man with the knowledge and understanding of a white; he was also a Cheyenne, with the lore of ancient rites deeply implanted in him, and the welfare of his people at heart.

Old Beaver spun about, darting to his tepee, snatching up the flag. He emerged almost at a run, carrying it high, and as he came into view he stumbled, one foot catching in a dragging fold of the cloth and all but tripping him. The flag waved wildly, enveloping him, and a couple of old men, seeing the mishap, rushed forward to his aid.

To them it was a regrettable accident, nothing more. To Captain Schmitt, watching suspiciously as he approached, it had the look of a sudden attack from the spurious shelter of the flag. Having been alert for something of the sort, he needed nothing more.

The ensuing moments ran wild with carnage. The blue lines swept forward, guns blazing, swords flashing. There was no bugle sounding a charge, nothing but disorder which degenerated swiftly into a melee. In it, men rode through the camp, firing wherever a target presented itself, men as suddenly as volatile and excited as dogs scenting a prey, yelling, stabbing slashing. Tepees crashed to earth under the onslaught. Wailing women and weeping children ran wildly, and a few arrows were loosed, but as indiscriminately as the attack and even more at random.

Within a tenth of an hour the encampment had ceased to exist, decimated as if by the passing of a tornado. Only then did Overton, shouting hoarsely, manage to halt the slaughter, to bring a semblance of order, his fury venting itself upon all who came within range. Confronting Schmitt, he was raging.

"What is the meaning of this, Mr. Schmitt? Who gave you permission to order an attack?"

Schmitt stared, then saluted. No trace of a smile was allowed to play at the corners of his mouth.

"Permission?" he countered. "None was given me. I gave no order. I supposed that it came from you—"

Apparently no order had been given, but Schmitt had led the men, and Overton, looking about, was sickened rather than appeased. His command had gone into action, and they had emerged from it victorious and almost unscathed. Conversely, they had slaughtered like a pack of foxes let loose in a henyard.

A child lay as though asleep, looking up from sightless eyes. A squaw, running to throw herself protectingly above him, had been all but decapitated by the wild stroke of a sword. Chief Old Beaver, still tangled in the folds of the flag, had a mingled look of hopelessness and incredulity. The white bands of cloth were red from blood spilling from a wound above his heart.

That was only a small part of the whole. At least half a hundred had gone down, the majority of them women and children. Here and there one still stirred or moaned, but most were still. Those who could had fled.

The hideousness of what he had allowed hit Overton like the flat of a sword. It was not so much the dead or the dying, the unprovoked attack, but its manner which concerned him. Captain Schmitt was replying to him with a bland calmness which contrasted with his own wild shouting, and suddenly Overton was silent. This had happened, and he was the commander, responsible for his officers and men as well as for his own decisions.

If he allowed it to become known that such a thing could take place under his eyes, without his approval and contrary to his orders, he would be forever disgraced, his career at an end. Since he was responsible, he must acknowledge it, and he might as well accept the credit instead of taking the blame.

Most of the ordinary citizenry across the country, from Massachusetts merchants to California miners, had rallied to the cry of a manifest destiny; the press applauded victories but had small patience with defeat. How this affair would rank would depend upon him.

He swallowed, resisting the impulse to brush a sleeve across his face. Instead, he settled his feet more firmly in the stirrups.

"Of course, Mr. Schmitt," he said formally. "In the confusion, my instructions were not properly relayed to you, but you behaved properly." He jerked nervously at a gunshot, glancing sidewise involuntarily. A soldier had finished off a squaw as a gesture of mercy. Then, as the man dismounted and a knife flashed in the light, Overton added harshly:

"But let there be no mutilation of victims. See to it."

Captain Schmitt saluted and swung to check the trooper. This will teach them a lesson, he thought, and broadened the idea to include not alone the Indians but such men in blue as had shown themselves increasingly antagonistic to himself or his methods. For now those methods were official; their conduct was a result of the orders of Overton.

Order was restored, the officers enforcing it on reluctant men. Zimmerman assisted, willing to do that. Since his superiors had given the orders, he could neither halt nor countermand them, but he had held himself aloof, wanting no part in such a business.

In the sudden silence, a man came riding, his horse moving at a slow walk. Not until he was almost in front of him did Overton recognize Lieutenant Bentley. The mask-like look of his face, the rigidity with which he held himself, gave him the appearance of a stranger.

He pulled up, not bothering to salute, possibly because one hand held the bridle reins, while the fingers of his other crossed upon the saddle-horn.

"Damn you, Overton," he said hoarsely, and the strain under which he had been laboring as the miles of march increased became suddenly apparent. "Look upon your handiwork and take pride in the murderous beast that you are! Slaughter, massacre of the innocents, of women and children and old men, even of friends beneath the cover of their country's flag—"

He checked, drawing a deep, sighing breath, then went on, as others stood numbed by the shock of such insubordination and plain speaking.

"It was unprovoked and without justification. I suppose your excuse was manifest destiny! Must our country build upon such foundations of decay—"

Overton had listened, as taken aback as anyone. Momentarily, recognizing the justification, he had remained speechless. Now rage swelled past the block.

"Silence, sirrah! Have you lost your senses? Captain Schmitt, place this man under arrest—"

He broke off as Bentley swayed, his desperate grip on the horn loosening. He slid and toppled, to sprawl, face uppermost, eyes suddenly glassy. Only then was the arrow which transfixed him from breast to back revealed by a spurting gush of blood. Broken, the shaft had been hidden by the rumpled shirt.

12.

Overton's face whitened as if covered by sudden snow. He stared down at the betraying shaft, the picture suddenly clearing, assuming new and ironic proportions. It had required no particular ability to foresee the trend of events, but it had taken courage on the part of a junior officer to raise his voice in protest, as Bentley had done.

When the clash had come about, he had ridden at his post, clearly hating it, taking no part in the shooting, but obeying orders. Swept through the village, caught up in the frenzied charge, he had been afforded a comprehensive view of the carnage, while helpless to alter the course of events.

Apparently he was the only casualty among those who wore the blue. An arrow loosed in desperation had found a target, and he had known that he was dying as he voiced his protest, denouncing Overton because of what had happened. Overton looked, feeling as though the arrow had transfixed his own heart. In the past days he had come to feel an unwilling respect, almost a liking, for this new and very junior officer.

Schmitt was staring down as well, almost as startled. He had despised Bentley, considering his protests more a cover for cowardice than an expression of conviction. It was jarring to realize that he had been wrong, that even in his final moments Bentley had not been railing against the injustice which had overtaken him but against the slaughter of the innocents. Right or wrong, he had been no coward.

Overton was out of the saddle, kneeling beside Bentley, striving with a desperate sense of futility to hold back reality. But the lieutenant was dead. That the arrow had found its target in a friend rendered it no less lethal.

The wonder was that Bentley had lived even a few minutes with the shaft transfixing him. It had been driven by a strong hand, at point-blank range. Overton got tiredly to his feet.

"Have a grave prepared," he instructed. "We will give him a military funeral, with as many honors as the circumstances permit." He stared across the camp, as devastated as the smaller one had been a few days before. They had had an easy victory there, as was to be expected, but his initial reaction was altering. Such a slaughter should teach the Indians that it was dangerous to arouse the wrath of the army; and that lesson, taken to heart, could be of value.

But he was seeing details which had escaped him in the first confused rush. Meat was scattered about from one end of the camp to the other, where it had been in the process of preparation, from whole, freshly slaughtered animals to sliced and drying strips. He could still make out where portions had been mixed with berries to make pemmican. The place had been a factory, with a big crew hard at work.

Within minutes, the accumulated food from many weeks of effort had been destroyed or fouled. Those who had died swiftly were very likely the lucky ones.

The long-range consequences of cold and hunger left him unmoved. But the short-term possibilities of the act were disturbing. The word would go out, spreading faster than a galloping horse could carry it, to the hunters still afield. It would transform them into warriors, with a fresh and savage purpose.

It would be the part of discretion to head back for the fort, not to waste time needlessly. But another part of his mind refused to be moved. It was fitting that Lieutenant Bentley, as the only army casualty, should be buried where he had fallen, his body commemorating the field of battle. And because of the manner of his death, those angry words thrown at him, which rankled now in Overton's mind, reparation must be made to the fullest degree within his power.

A detail was set to digging. Beasley superintended

the preparation of the body, extracting the broken
halves of the arrow with his own hands. His glance
shifted inquiringly to the others who had perished
in the encounter, stiffening forms lying scattered and
neglected.

"How about them?" he asked. "Are they to receive
no burial?"

Sergeant O'Reilly, swearing over the removal of an
obtrusively large stone from the grave, turned to
stare in amazement.

"You mean dig holes for them, Lieutenant? Be too
big a job—and anyway, why should we?"

Beasley did not answer, for O'Reilly's reply was
sufficiently revealing. And certainly he, unlike Bentley, was old enough in the service to cherish few
illusions.

Captain Schmitt selected an honor guard to fire
a volley above the grave. True to his promise, Major
Overton was omitting nothing of pomp and splendor
for one of their own. Deserved honors, unquestionably, but Beasley had a feeling that Bentley, even
if he could know, would not appreciate the ceremony.

O'Reilly climbed from the pit, dusting himself
carelessly, then carried word to where Overton
waited, nervously thumbing a prayer book which
was always packed among his supplies for the trail.
The absence of a chaplain disturbed him. He wanted
every part of this, including the ceremony, to be as

perfect as possible. It was the least as well as the last thing that he could do for Bentley, and he had the uncomfortable feeling that he owed it to the dead man.

Everything was in readiness, the officers drawn up in the forefront, the men farther back, in precise formation, the honor guard at the edge. Major Overton took his place, his glance ranging mechanically over the details. The half opened book closed with a snap as his eyes narrowed.

"Mr. McChesney," he said sharply. "Where is he?"

Somehow, incredibly, no one had seemed to notice until then. There had been so much action, so much confusion and such a tangled stream of emotion in the minds of nearly everyone that his absence had gone unnoticed. Anger, never far below the surface, boiled in Overton. But his voice was icily controlled.

"Find and bring him. His presence is required at such an occasion. And if he's sulking, boycotting this as a means of protest—"

The last words were spoken below his breath, but their harshness was revealed by the rasp of his tones. He had been very patient with everyone, but there was a limit to his good nature. He was about ready to make an example—

A deeper red surged in his cheeks as his eyes dropped to the canvas-wrapped body; the red of shame rather than anger. He'd been on the point of making an example of Bentley—

The day, rawly gloomy, was fast drawing to evening. After the shroud of grayness, the clouds showed signs of breaking, and a lance of sunshine touched the dirt, mounded at either side. It might almost have been a benediction, but the effect was spoiled by the angry bawling of Captain Schmitt, detailing men to the search.

The beginning movement halted, with head turning, eyes staring. One man's jaws hung agape. As though in response to Overton's command, Mike McChesney was coming.

If his approach was tardy, that was explained at least in part as he appeared over a small hill at one extreme of the camp ground, no longer riding but on foot. He moved steadily but slowly, and that too was understandable as they saw what burden he carried in both arms. Whether it was a body or someone sick or wounded was not immediately apparent, but he bore it tenderly.

His absence up to then was explained, and there was nothing very surprising in it. He too had ridden with the rest, in his proper place as an officer, swept along by the tide. Like Bentley, he had felt sickened and outraged, helpless and revolted, but it had not been a matter of choice.

Afterward, if he chose to have a look around, that was both his privilege and his responsibility. It came to Overton, again instilling a sense of uneasiness, that he had neglected certain duties, shocked by what had happened to Bentley, perhaps taking too much for granted. McChesney, without orders but requiring none, had been guilty of no such omission.

He had found someone or something—

His face was gray, mask-like, but otherwise devoid of expression. What forces might boil just below the surface were held under iron control.

He came on steadily, slowed but not greatly hampered by his burden, and now every pair of eyes could make out, with a mounting sense of horror mixed with incredulity, what it was he had found. It was a woman, lying limp and slender, head falling back over his right arm, throat exposed, and, like the face above, milk-white under the sudden touch of sun. The blue eyes were open but staring on vacancy. Hair of a soft brownish-gold hung in disorder about her face.

She was unmistakably a white woman, and just as surely out of place in this far corner of the frontier. She wore a cloak, unbuttoned and fallen open to reveal a white shirt waist which once had been starched and frilly. Now the edge, like the sleeve about the left arm, hanging below McChesney's, carried a wide brown stain. Even without the sightless quality of her gaze, there would have been no need to ask if the girl lived.

Overton watched as McChesney approached, his glance held by the woman's face, and he shivered as if with sudden cold. Here was one more in a lengthening list of incomprehensible incidents, part of a train which he had allowed to be set in motion, happenings neither planned nor intended. This was the face of a woman as beautiful as she was young, as innocent as the bewilderment which some days back had dwelt in the eyes of Lieutenant Bentley.

Overton's mind leaped like a pouncing puma. There could be only one answer, and it would be the justification for all that had happened. Precisely how or why was not important, in the fact of stark reality. McChesney halted a few paces back from the grave, still holding his burden, his eyes ranging understandingly to the preparations and devoid of emotion. Overton exclaimed angrily:

"What's this you've found, Mr. McChesney? A white woman—and of course she was a captive, murdered as we approached—"

McChesney's negative shake of the head checked his tirade. Overton had been on the verge of denouncing all Indians as treacherous and murderous, terms which in his belief were fully justified. Yet those were akin to the words which Bentley had flung at him with his last breath.

"A white woman, yes," McChesney agreed, and glanced down at the still face so near his own, his voice harsh and strident. "And murdered, as you say—but not by the Indians, Major. Not by any of these poor unfortunates who clustered under the flag and depended upon it for the protection which was denied them."

"But I don't understand—"

"It's really quite simple, in light of what has happend. I chanced to be where I could see—I was afforded an excellent view, in fact, though from a distance, and I tried to get to them, to interpose myself, to stop or prevent the carnage which was taking place. Unfortunately, I was too far away."

Overton, like the others, was silent, beginning to sense McChesney's meaning, waiting with growing apprehension.

"She was with several others—squaws, if you wish to call them that—other women, children, a couple of old men. They are all still there, where they went down. They were standing under or around the flag, unarmed, terrified, but putting their trust in it—and in the honor of a government which, like them, had been betrayed. I witnessed how they were shot down, this woman along with the rest—by men of your command, Major. Massacred, yes, but not by savage red men; but by even more savage whites!"

13.

McChesney delivered the accusation firmly but without heat; it was as though he were holding still stronger emotions in check by a supreme effort. Overton fought a feeling of sickness. That such a thing could have happened was shocking, almost past comprehension. His suddenly blurted words sounded inane, even in his own ears.

"And we don't even know who she was!"

"But we do, Major. She is my sister."

Overton goggled, striving to comprehend, to adjust his thinking to the shock of this fresh knowledge. He remembered what McChesney had told him, that his sister was coming to that country to visit him at the fort, and that McChesney expected then to return East with her. There had been something about an uncle, a mill and its management.

That McChesney's sister should make such a journey had been unusual, bordering on the extraordinary, but that she should have arrived at such a time, coming by way of Twin Buttes at the time of this clash near their feet, was even more unexpected—though he had heard somewhere that the stage road ran somewhere in the vicinity—

He caught himself, conscious that he was trying to find excuses in his own mind, that the only odd part of the proceeding was that she should have arrived at that point at so fatal a moment. And yet that was not so strange. Despite the unrest of the past weeks, the stagecoach had continued to make its tri-weekly run, after he had given his personal assurance as commandant that there was nothing to fear.

But conditions had changed during the past several days, since a watcher on a butte had been killed, a small unimportant camp wiped out. He had refused to admit that such conduct might have a bearing on the situation, yet now the impact and the effect was clear. The Cheyennes had acted, stopping the stage, making prisoners of its occupants. Almost desperately he grasped at that straw.

"You mean that the Indians had taken her prisoner, that they had attacked the stage—"

McChesney shook his head, a slow motion but completely negative.

"Any such assumption is unjustified by the evidence, Major. The stage coach was wrecked, but almost certainly not from an attack."

Anger was coming to Overton's rescue. Bad as the situation had been, it was steadily worsening, and he had to strike out against the net which was closing about him. "And how can you be sure of that, sirrah? he countered. "If it was wrecked, as you say—"

He broke off as McChesney turned, moving a few steps, gently easing his burden to the ground against the dirt mounded at one side of the grave. The pale face of the dead woman seemed to stare accusingly, but of her fair, frail beauty there could be no question. McChesney's face worked, and he blinked rapidly. Then, with rigid control, he swung back.

"What basis have you for so extraordinary a statement in regard to the stage being wrecked?" Overton demanded. "I appreciate your feelings, sir, and you have my deepest sympathy. But you are indulging in sweeping assumptions. If she was with those Indians, it must have been as a captive—"

Again, with no more than a lifted hand, Mike cut him short. The hand was stained with blood, and Overton stared at the smear as though fascinated.

"I reached her side shortly after she was killed," McChesney explained. "By then, those who were able to get away had done so, though they were being pursued—"

He checked his voice on a rising note of anger, reverting to a factual account of his own actions

"I saw at once that she was past any help Also, I was a prey to some of the doubts and questions which you have raised. So I did some looking around, trying to find answers. I came upon an old man, badly wounded—from the stab of a sword. He was too proud to beg, too certain that he would be shown no mercy in any case, but from the look in his eyes I knew how much he craved a drink. The wounded dying are often tormented by thirst."

Overton nodded his understanding. Experience on battlefields, after carnage, had taught him that.

"I found water and gave him a drink, and he revived momentarily. I asked him about the white woman, and he said the stagecoach came past yesterday, and something had gone wrong in full view of those in the camp. Horses and coach all went over a cliff, where the road skirts one of the buttes. Everyone on board was killed except her."

He indicated his sister with a nod, his voice tight.

"She had hardly been hurt. The old man pointed the spot out to me before he died."

Like the others, Schmitt had been listening tensely. Now he interrupted:

"A likely story on their part! Why would a stage be wrecked at such a spot unless it was attacked? Of course they massacred the others. Since she was a woman, they made her captive—"

McChesney's gaze swung, and at something in his eyes, Schmitt fell silent.

"What you have suggested semed to me a likely possibility," Mike granted. "But it was easy to check the story, at least in part. I went over and looked. The wreckage of the stagecoach lies at the base of the cliff. The coach was so badly smashed that it is a wonder that anyone could have survived the plunge, but strange things happen. She lived—to be killed today."

"That was unfortunate," Schmitt granted. "But I don't see that the stage being badly smashed in any way disproves that there was an attack upon it."

"That could have happened—except that the old man, dying, assured me that it was not that way."

"And you take the word of an Indian?" Schmitt was incredulous.

"He was dying, Captain."

Schmitt opened his mouth, then shrugged. "I suppose there's no way of knowing for sure now."

"On the contrary, it will be a simple matter to check the truth. There are three new, shallow graves, not far from the wreckage, at the bottom of a small coulee. Indians do not make a practice of burying their victims—but they had buried those men."

"If they did, then it was to conceal the evidence of their butchery," Schmitt insisted. "I know how the red devils operate."

"The facts will be easy to discover," McChesney pointed out. "The bodies can easily be examined. And what better time than now?" He glanced toward Overton.

The major shrugged heavily. *Damn him,* he thought. *Damn them both.* Schmitt had blundered, desperate at the turn events had taken. Overton was faced with the stark realization that the man had a propensity for blundering, for contriving disaster. And McChesney, coming upon his sister in such fashion—certainly Overton sympathized with him, though for him to be proven right was rubbing salt in a wound.

He nodded heavily to O'Reilly.

"Proceed with your shovel men at Mr. McChesney's instructions, Sergeant."

They trooped across to the rise of the nearer butte, actually more a long bluff ending abruptly, with cliffs on two sides. The road followed its crest before swinging to descend, hardly a stone's throw beyond where it had missed the turn and gone off. The wreckage lay scattered.

McChesney indicated the long, shallow mounds in a nearby coulee. Only a little work was required to disinter the bodies, who were revealed as white men, clearly the victims of the accident.

Overton had followed along, disliking this increasingly, yet impelled, knowing what they must find.

McChesney's sureness had been convincing. That the Cheyennes would bury the men was proof.

All had been badly hurt in the tumbling fall of the stagecoach and instantly killed. That a woman passenger should survive almost unhurt had been a freak of luck.

The injuries to the men had clearly resulted from the fall, not from arrows or bullets. Nor had the dead been mutilated.

Speechless for once, Schmitt stared. The very muteness of these dead was an accusation. The Cheyennes of this camp had been friendly, and they had demonstrated their good will as tangibly as possible.

At McChesney's nod, O'Reilly gave the order to reinter the dead, then to pack heavy stones from a pile at the bottom of the cliff, to cover the mounds against digging by animals. Overton led the way back to the other grave.

His face was haggard, pale beneath the tan. But darkness was not far off. What remained to be done had to be finished quickly. He looked uncertainly at McChesney.

"I'm sorry, McChesney—more than I can say. This has been a ghastly mistake—"

He swallowed and went on huskily:

"She—your sister—must be buried also. What is your wish? Do you desire a separate grave—or shall we take her body back to the fort?"

McChesney had been considering, his mind coldly mechanical as he held down the emotions which could so easily burst out of control. It had been a mistake of the gravest proportions, not only for Martha, but for others who had been virtual by-standers, caught by surprise, swept up in a senseless act, the mania of a glory-hunter.

But nothing could change what had happened or restore the dead. Worse, though that seemed hard to believe, this folly might well have set in motion forces which would wash the far reaches of the plains as the ripple from a thrown rock spreads to the limits of a pool. Overton and Schmitt were too self-centered, too ignorant of the forces with which they dealt, really to understand what they had done. But Orlando Overton was beginning to sense it.

"I think that we should complete the burial and get out of here as soon as possible," he said. "Word will be carried to the hunters, and they will lose no time before heading back, thirsting for vengeance. A second massacre at this spot will hardly profit any-one, especially a fresh list of victims.

"Where she lies will make no difference to Martha —now. If she knew, she would perhaps be honored to share a grave with Mr. Bentley—as they share a common fate."

Overton swallowed again, nodding. "It is little

enough that we can do," he acknowledged. "Let's get on with it, then."

They moved out in the closing dusk, horses and men at a quickening tempo. There was nothing to fear, of course. They were too strong a force for that, and Schmitt felt comfortably assured that they had taught the savages a necessary lesson. Nonetheless, a feeling of distance was reassuring, and some at least took note that they had swung sharply and were heading back toward the fort.

14.

It was better luck than the army deserved or had a right to hope for: they moved steadily toward Lookout with no swerve or deviation. Indian sign was all about, visible in smoke rising against the sky, near or far, revealed in the tracks of many horsemen on the move, a portent in the air after the manner of an approaching storm. There were others, smaller yet more significant signs, visible to McChesney though unnoticed by the others.

But they suffered no attack, no delay or hindrance. That would be the fate of the uninvolved, the scattered settlers, smaller groups less able to defend themselves.

Overton made no effort to circle about to rescue or protect these settlers, not even to give them warning. He seemed obsessed with getting back to the fort, and they made it in three days; days in which the weather cleared and brought sharp sunshine with a blanketing frost at night. It was a breather before the onset of winter, bushes flaunting gold and beginning to fling these riches to the wind with a prodigal hand.

McChesney moved mechanically, his mind like the season, in a state of suspension. His hurt was bitter but deep; for the moment it must be controlled. As long as he wore the uniform, he would serve it without dishonor. But a dream lay buried, along with his sister, both needless casualties.

Inside his own quarters, a room with which he had barely had time to become acquainted since being transferred there, he looked about, fingering the calendar on one wall. It was a heritage from a predecessor, probably, he suspected, a treasured memento given out by a drugstore from a small town in Maryland. The smiling eyes of a girl looked warmly down, as though belying the slow march of time which the months clutched so reluctantly.

The date, verified, was as he remembered. His period of enlistment had expired a week before.

It fell upon a Wednesday, in mid-week; a week not merely wasted, but tragically so.

He bathed and shaved, changing to a clean uniform. Ordinarily he luxuriated in such a task, the washing away not only of grime but of weariness, of frustrations and the accumulated rigors of the miles. Today his body was like his mind, without feeling.

He intended to have a final interview with Overton, one not quite according to the book. After that he'd be free.

The trouble was that now he had nowhere to go, no purpose. Without Martha, he might not return East.

An orderly brought a message. Major Overton requested his presence.

"I'll go with you," he said. Whatever Overton wanted, if he was hoping to forestall him in his decision, it was too late. Until a few days before, he would have continued on, if not happy in his career at least feeling a measure of contentment. Now that, like the rest, was a casualty.

He was startled at Overton's appearance. The major had kept increasingly aloof during the return trip, and McChesney had not seen him for a couple of days. Slumped now in a chair behind a desk, Overton looked sick. He tried to draw himself more erect, not quite succeeding. He gestured toward another chair.

"Please be seated, Lieutenant. I'm not quite myself today."

Whether his illness was of the mind or the flesh, he certainly looked sick. McChesney almost felt a pang of pity. Unquestionably the sweep had proved an ordeal for Overton.

"You reminded me the other day that your enlistment was up," Overton went on, and McChesney's resolution hardened at this attempt to forestall him. "I have not forgotten."

"It was up last week," McChesney said. "And so request an immediate discharge."

"You shall have it, sir, as is your right." Overton did not make the mistake of asking what he might do now, to expose himself to a devastating answer. First, however, I have a request—a favor to ask of you—that you will remain in the service a few days longer, to undertake a mission of great importance. I would not ask it except that there is no one else to whom I can turn—no one to whom I would entrust such a responsibility."

McChesney waited. Whatever it was, he would refuse, and once out of uniform, he intended to tell Overton, in precise terms, exactly what he thought of him. But that satisfaction would lose nothing for being deferred.

"When we talked together some days ago, you told me of your sister's expected arrival for a visit, and mentioned that Miss Trout, the daughter of Colonel Trout, was also coming. I bitterly regret what happened to your sister. That, and the needless death of Lieutenant Bentley, have haunted me."

There was no doubting his sincerity. These dead were of his race, and so of concern to him. His almost complete indifference to what happened to others was not deliberate callousness. His credo, manifest destiny for the white man, allowed of no deviation. A way had to be cleared across a wilderness, so those who stood in the path must be swept aside.

In that there was no room for an all-embracing sympathy, and to him such a thing was out of place.

McChesney had come to know him almost too well. Here was a man at once likeable yet dangerous, sure in his convictions but not trusting his own judgment. His eagerness to debate, to argue not alone the opinions of others but his own, showed his weakness. That, in one entrusted with command, could be serious.

"A despatch was waiting when I returned," Overton went on. "I am informed that Miss Trout is on her way, so it is too late to stop her or for her to turn back, despite the turn which events have taken. She travels with a strong escort, coming, as you are probably aware, from the north. I am requested to have her met at Plimpton's Wells, to escort her the rest of the way."

McChesney nodded. The Wells were a three-day journey from Fort Lookout. "I've been there," he conceded.

"Then you know the country. I realize that it is asking a lot, especially under the circumstances, but I want you to head the escort and make sure of her safe arrival; to march with East Company and as soon as possible, since she should already be at the Wells by the time you can hope to arrive."

Mike regarded him with a bemused incredulity. The colonel's daughter had set out, according to plan, unaware of what had taken place at Two Buttes. Had her father known, he would certainly have vetoed any journey for the present. With such a threat over the land, Overton in turn ought to turn her back at the Wells out of concern for her safety.

But that was his business. It was not for McChesney to point out his stupidity.

"Under normal circumstances, I would prefer to go myself, but that is out of the question," Overton continued. "For the last several miles I was barely able to remain in the saddle. I hope to be sufficiently recovered to welcome her fittingly when she comes, but I'm not up to going."

There could be no doubt as to that point. He looked on the verge of collapse.

"What about Captain Schmitt?"

"After what has happened?" Overton gestured wearily. "As commander, I am responsible for what has happened—but I don't want to be saddled with an added responsibility. Captain Schmitt knows just one thing: how to fight. Normally that is right and proper for a soldier, but he is too indiscriminate. Would you entrust the colonel's daughter to his care under existing conditions?"

With Schmitt eliminated, that left it up to one of the lieutenants, and of those, McChesney was the senior and also the more experienced. For such a chore, with the danger of attack an ever-present threat—

"You see why I ask you," Overton went on. "I will esteem it a favor, and so, I know, will Colonel Trout. Once you have returned, you will be free to go if you wish. But such an interlude should not prove too onerous."

Normally it was an assignment at which any officer would leap. Margaret Trout was not only a colonel's daughter, but she had been born and bred to the frontier. McChesney had heard of her, as who had not? She was noted to be something of a beauty, as inured to the saddle and hardship as a man, yet a charming companion.

"I realize how ironic this is for you," Overton added. "But she must be met. It is too late to make any change."

With East Company for an escort, he could not be accused of holding back. McChesney shrugged. He would do it for the lady, not for Overton. A few days would make no difference, since he had nothing in mind once he doffed the uniform.

East Company grumbled, almost with a sense of outrage. They had been longer than usual on extended duty, had barely returned to the comparative luxury of the fort. Normally they would be permitted a rotation of rest before another similar assignment.

But this time, as in the case of McChesney, they recognized that there was little choice. Overton, when setting out, had largely stripped the garrison for his expedition. He had picked up reinforcements as planned along the way, but they too had been long on the trail.

Once they were outfitted and ready, McChesney addressed them.

"You don't like this," he said bluntly, and refrained from adding that, if it came to a matter of choice, he didn't much like it, either. They were seasoned troops, but they had shown themselves to be glory-hunters, trigger-happy. That was largely the fault of their officers, for men reacted according to the leadership they received. On the whole they were well fitted for the trip.

"We're all tired, and we'll be moving at a steady pace. There may or may not be fighting. I hope to avoid any clashes, but some may be forced on us.

"I've observed you in action, and you can take it. We're going to meet Miss Margaret Trout and escort her back here. She is the daughter of Colonel Malcolm Trout. Since she is already on her way, we can't let a lady down."

Seldom did their officers condescend to explain what lay ahead, or why. A subtle change ran through the column. He hadn't been mistaken in telling them. Maggie Trout belonged to the regiment, her father's regiment, and beyond that, to the army. Tired they might be, but no longer disgruntled. They would fight if necessary to reach her, fight their way back to insure her safety.

There was a moon, and they made the most of it,

heading north until it blinked below the horizon. McChesney chose his sentries with care, posting them himself, then slept heavily. He was desperately tired, but that was good. It helped not to think, not to remember.

There had been no sign of Jim McGillicuddy since they had neared Two Buttes and he had gone on ahead. Showing unusual forbearance, Overton had asked no questions. Schmitt had growled something about a treacherous half-breed, but no one had really been surprised. He had been conscripted against his will to serve as a scout, but he had performed his duties ably, giving accurate reports, voicing a warning and proffering advice which, if heeded, might have made a vital difference.

Since he was a cousin to Running Wolf, the Cheyenne, and his brothers were with them, no one had really expected him to return after what had taken place. It was with some surprise that, at high noon of the following day, McChesney made out a lone rider, who, nearing, turned out to be the scout.

He greeted McChesney casually, showing no surprise. Clearly the Cheyennes were well informed.

"I take it that you're meeting Miss Trout?"

With such a man there was no point in dissembling. Besides, McChesney liked and respected him and had a feeling that it was reciprocal.

"That's right."

McGillicuddy grunted.

"The major made one sensible descision. I was afraid he'd send Schmitt—and if he had, nothing could have prevented them from being wiped out. But I once had the pleasure of meeting Maggie Trout. For her sake, also your sister's and your own— if you keep your men under discipline, there will be no trouble, going or. coming."

"I appreciate that, Jim." McChesney extended his hand. He understood what such a pledge meant, and how the scout must have labored to obtain it. Whatever Schmitt might term him, he was fair-minded and generous.

"Mind you, it extends no farther," Jim warned. "Also, some may not have had the word or feel bound by it. There is always danger."

"I understand. And you?"

"We probably will not meet again. From now on, I fight with my own people—the Cheyenne."

15.

Plimpton's Wells formed a man-made oasis in the middle of a dry stretch of country. For some reason obscure to others than himself, George Plimpton had determined to settle there, but water was a requisite. Having been a well-digger by trade, Plimpton had turned his hand to finding water, digging a deep but dry hole, then trying again at a little distance with the same distressing lack of result. Only then had he abandoned the project and departed for parts unknown.

Not long afterward, a lone rider had stopped unwillingly at the thirsty insistence of his horse, surprised at the instinct of the cayuse and startled to find both wells not only filled to the brim with water but overflowing in small streams which soon lost themselves in the surrounding dryness. What had caused the gushers, belatedly confirming Plimpton's instinct, no one knew. But the water was there.

That, at least, was the expectation, and Plimpton's Wells had become a stopping place for travelers of all descriptions. On this occasion they marked a half-way point between the two forts, a convenient place for meeting.

Those from the north were ahead of them. Mc-Chesney had made them out from a distance, grazing horses, blue-clad figures lounging, a single pitched tent, and a high-wheeled, unlovely vehicle, an army ambulance. It marked the best which could be provided for the transportation of the colonel's daughter, affording shade from a too warm sun, shelter from snow or driving rain. Beyond that its advantages over a horse and saddle were debatable.

The escort was only a quarter of the size sent by Overton, deemed adequate under the conditions which had existed when they had set out, prior to news of the clash at Two Buttes. Since they had certainly been under the observation of Cheyenne scouts, McChesney ascribed their safety to the fair-mindedness of James McGillicuddy.

What he had heard of the colonel's daughter was true. Instead of waiting demurely in her tent for him to be announced, she was outside with the others, watching as eagerly as any, a slender, neatly gowned figure, brown hair crowned by a small perky hat which unquestionably had come from some shop well to the east of the big river. Matching brown eyes appraised him as he alighted, and she held out a hand, soft but firm, well browned by the sun, smiling as though pleased. McChesney struggled with a sudden shortness of breath, his eyes drinking her in. Oasis was the proper, the only word for this place with her to grace it.

He had not known quite what to expect, but Margaret Trout went beyond his best imaginings. She moved with the easy litheness, the grace of a well-trained soldier, but there was nothing mannish about her ease and graciousness; rather a complete feminnity, which would have graced a drawing room. In spite of that, she was at home amid the wildness of her surroundings. Her voice was as he had sensed that it would be, soft yet clear, reminding him of the ripple of a stream.

"You arrive precisely on schedule, Lieutenant—" Her eyes held a fleeting surprise, as though faintly bewildered that he was not a younger man. "And most welcome, of course."

She was extending her hand, and Mike took it, pleased again at the gesture, the firmness of her clasp, doffing his own hat with his free hand.

"Lieutenant McChesney, ma'am. You are generous." By rights they should have been there to meet her. He explained that briefly. "We returned rather tardily from an extended scout, which Major Overton had led. The despatch concerning you had arrived ahead of us."

"Then you did doubly well to come so soon." Her eyes questioned him. "And the major? Your scout was rewarding, I trust?"

"There were clashes along the way." He did not elaborate. "The tribes are increasingly restless. Major Overton deemed it prudent to remain at his post of command."

How much of her inquiry was inspired by politeness, how much by personal interest, he wondered. But Overton would be better pleased, in any case, if he said as little as possible. By the time they returned, he should be rested, recovered from the sickness which had gripped him.

It was a sickness, McChesney suspected, more of the mind than flesh. The tragedy which had overtaken Martha McChesney and Lieutenant Bentley had hit hard.

Another woman emerged from the tent. Mrs. Gallagher was probably a perfect companion for such a journey, but the necessity for the ambulance was explained. Her ample figure would more than fill a saddle.

With the men from both directions hungry for news, those from the north were quickly filled in regarding recent events in which East Company had played a part. McChesney was not surprised that those tidings should reach Maggie Trout's ears before the day was done. Though she was treated with utmost respect, both as the colonel's daughter and for her own sake, she was in their eyes an accepted part of the regiment, counting the men as friends, given whatever news they acquired.

Supper had been more of an occasion than usual, but it was out of the way, the men at ease save for the watch, dusk closing over the wide sweep of the land. The day had been warmly pleasant, so that the recent harsh weather seemed like a memory.

Margaret Trout had acquired a considerable fund of information regarding Lookout and what had happened during the recent sweep. McChesney was co-operative, but she noticed that of himself he said almost nothing.

"I've been told about your sister," she said. "I can't tell you how sorry I am."

Sympathy brought a deep note to her voice, expressing even more than the words. Mike's iron control wavered.

"It hit me hard," he confessed. "I hadn't seen her for so long, and I had been looking forward to it. The worst part was that it was all so useless, so unnecessary."

Normally he would not have spoken so plainly, as an officer, to a girl on such brief acquaintance. But he was no longer obligated to the service, and this woman was all that report had said and more. She was no longer a name, but a person, and he was aroused from his apathy, torn by apprehension. Chance had dictated that Martha should arrive in the country at a bad time, and for Maggie it might be no better.

"She was about your age," he added, "five years

my junior. I still can't quite accept that it has happened."

"You said it was unnecessary?"

"Worse than that. The whole business was a tragic mistake. Captain Schmitt exercises no restraint where Indians are concerned. Since my enlistment has expired, I'm free to speak."

"Oh." She was quick to understand his thought, with all the implications. Clearly he was not signing up again, was cutting off his career in mid-term. This was a double tragedy.

"I'm sorry," she repeated.

"I've told you this so that you will understand what I'm going to add," he went on. "When the arrangements were made for your visit, the Indians were hunting game. Now the nature of their hunt is changing. Lookout is well manned, but it might be more prudent to postpone your visit."

The loss of his sister gave him a right to speak. She considered it, not taking offense. Her headshake was grave.

"I appreciate your concern, Lieutenant. And I know something of your record, your experience. But this other is not so simple. If my father was still at our post—"

She went on with news which surprised him. Colonel Trout was being promoted, recalled to the East. He and her mother had set out on the same day as herself, heading east instead of south, to make the trip by easy stages. They planned to do some visiting along the way.

Under the circumstances, even though such action might be prudent, she could hardly return to the fort; nor could she readily rejoin her folks.

"If Father had known of these developments, he would probably have agreed with you," she told him. "As it is, my trip had been planned for quite a while, and I feel I must go on. With such a force as you have, and yourself in command, I won't be at all apprehensive."

"What you have said alters the situation," McChesney admitted. "And I'm selfish enough to be pleased that we can go on together instead of having to say hello and goodbye. I was afraid that you might turn back."

He was a little startled at his own boldness, but her laugh was low, pleased. "I'm glad that you didn't really want to be rid of me," she agreed. "I'll be as little trouble as possible."

"You'd be no trouble, ever," he said, and was surprised again at the fervency of his declaration. Later, blinking up at the stars from his blanket, he admitted the truth to himself, somewhat startled at the realization but pleased. He'd heard of love at first sight, never quite convinced that it could be true, certain that it could not happen to him. Yet now it had.

Somehow, it seemed completely natural, as inevitable along the way as a landmark on the trail.

Across the years he'd known a number of women, some very attractive, but none had ever moved him as did this girl. When he had seen her he had known. It had been as simple as that, as sure. It was more than a feeling or a wish; it was a conviction, an abiding sense of having come home after long wandering.

She had been raised in the tradition of the army, but he sensed her understanding. He was through with the military as a career, though it would be simple enough to keep on if he wished. Fighting was probably necessary, and there would be more of it. But as an instrument of a doctrine of manifest destiny, obliged to exterminate a people so that others might occupy their land—rightly or wrongly, that was not for him.

He could still have a career, managing for his uncle, as he had planned with Martha; if not that, there would be something else. The new-found wonder eased a little the hurt of Martha's loss. The stars held a brightness beyond anything he'd ever noticed before.

Her smile next morning was warm, her greeting friendly. At least she had not been offended by his plain speaking. The two escorts took their opposite ways as soon as they had breakfasted, and McChesney was pleased that it was a three-day journey back to the fort. At the start, with an ingrained tiredness from the long expedition aching through his bones, he'd cursed the weary miles to be covered. Now they were a boon, one of the few which came to a man wearing the uniform and riding the endless reaches of the frontier.

In mid-morning, Maggie grew impatient with the jolting of her conveyance and, at his suggestion, changed eagerly to a saddle. For the remainder of the day they rode together, finding a surprising number of topics about which to talk, common interests not only from the army but in matters a great deal more far-reaching.

McChesney caught himself laughing, lifted out of himself from the despondency which had gripped him. He considered that, embarrassed, then decided that Martha would approve. He grieved for her no less, but life, like a river, coursed on, and like it or not, a man was carried with the current. Martha would want him to go on living, in the fuller meaning of the term; she would rejoice if he could find happiness.

Those days were in the nature of a vacation, and Maggie Trout seemed to enjoy them as much as he. What the men of Easy Company might think, McChesney could guess, but he did not care. He was circumspect, but if he enjoyed the company of a charming lady whom he was detailed to escort, there was nothing wrong in that.

They camped beside a stream the second evening, and he cut a willow pole, rigged a line and pulled out a trout, then, at the eagerness in Maggie's glance, gave it to her. She caught several more, a tasty addition to their supper.

The weather held, perfect for the season, with a warm sun by day, a moon and high stars by night. Neither climbed higher than his soaring hopes, his new-found dreams.

It was as Maggie was preparing to return to her tent that she found herself in his arms, and her lips were warm, responsive. He hadn't intended to kiss her, but it had been a compulsion, drawing them both. Then, as she drew back, her eyes were suddenly troubled.

"It must be the moon," she gasped. "Not that I regret it. That was very sweet, Mike. Only I see now that I should have told you sooner, but I never dreamed—"

Her eyes were as grave as her voice, tender but steady.

"You see—I'm visiting Fort Lookout because I'm supposed to marry Major Overton."

16.

Orlando Overton had told the truth. He had been sick, physically exhausted, and a prey to conflicting emotions. But knowing himself, he had been confident that a period of rest would put him back in shape, in proper condition to welcome Margaret Trout. It was largely a matter of composing his mind.

He was waiting, urbane and smiling, greeting her warmly but with a proper public reserve as the ambulance cramped its wheels and swung to a stop. Maggie flashed a quick, uncertain look at McChesney, her own poise shaken. The pain in his eyes the evening before had been too sharp to mistake, before he had succeeded in masking it. She had been afforded a revealing glimpse, which his careful courtesy and guarded reserve since then had in no way dispelled.

As a soldier's daughter and a lady, she had man-

aged an untroubled face for public view, keeping
back the tears while lying sleepless after her statement and partial confession—words which she had
felt impelled to speak, only too well aware of the
way Mike McChesney looked at her, the devotion in
his eyes. Of necessity it was a very sudden thing with
him, somewhat impossible and preposterous—except
that she understood only too well, her own emotions
responding similarly.

It had been the honorable thing, a necessary measure, and she had trod the thin edge of truth as carefully as possible. She was making this visit to Fort
Lookout because she was supposed to marry Orlando
Overton. He had been a guest at her father's post
a year before, intending to spend a night, lengthening his stay to a week, forced then to tear himself
away but proposing before he went.

In the intervening months, remembering him dis-
passionately, she had found him attractive, even
charming—and in retrospect, as in actuality, somewhat frightening. Unsure of herself, unable to sort
out her emotions but flattered by his attentions, she
had said neither yes nor no, and even after an exchange of letters everything was still tentative, something to be decided at a later date.

Her father's promotion and imminent departure
for the East had brought matters to a head. Overton had renewed his pleas, urging her to visit Look-

out, since he could not get away. The implication that by such an acceptance she would also accept him, with a quick wedding to follow rather than a return to her folks, was clear if unspoken.

But a decision had to be made; it was unfair to the major to keep him any longer in suspense, and she did like him. Marriage would solve a number of matters at this juncture in her life. She would see him again, and more than likely confirm what the visit implied.

Yet actually it was as she had said—she was supposed to marry Overton, but she had not agreed to do so. That second part she could not in modesty add, though it was only fair and honorable to warn McChesney as she had. The meeting with Overton was only hours away, and he would be both host and suitor, in addition to being commandant of the fort.

Until she had given him her answer she could not, in good conscience, say more to Mike, much as she was desirous of doing so. If, later, he still felt as she was certain that he did—

Perceptive as she was, even she could not guess what hell Mike endured that night and the following day. He had himself under control, and as the officer in charge of her escort he kept a tight rein on his emotions. He understood, or thought he did, her real feelings, along with the reasons for her visit to the fort. If he hadn't been blindly stupid, carried away by the onrush of his own feelings, he might have guessed.

She had been friendly, pleasant and warm-hearted, but she had been fair, warning him when it became necessary. She could hardly have done so earlier.

The day, traveling along with her, was torment. Bad enough as it was that she intended to marry such a man as Overton, whom he knew to be a weakling and not above being a scoundrel when his own desires warranted, his own loss was even more bitter. That he could lose what he had never possessed was not a point for debate. He had loved her, and, God help him, he would continue to love her.

The onrush of emotion, wholly new in his experience, had served as a balm for the loss of Martha. And now—

Now he was cast again to the depths. He would deliver her safely to the fort, as he was supposed to do. Thereafter, with as little loss of time as possible, he would shed his uniform and all connection with the army—

Beyond that was only blankness. Sudden dreams had turned to nightmares. He couldn't stay around where she was, certainly not see her become the wife of another man. But leaving her behind would not erase her from his mind or heart, and the trail ahead, uncertain and troubled before, would be twice as bitter.

Overton's mood, by contrast, was one of elation. She had responded to his invitation to visit the fort, constrained by the imminent separation of a couple of thousand additional miles, the need to make up her mind and marry him if she would. That she had chosen to come seemed a strong augury of her ultimate decision. The sight of her reinforced his own resolve. Not only was she the daughter of a colonel who would soon be a general, and therefore a most desirable father-in-law for an ambitious officer; she was fully as attractive in her own person as he remembered, the perfect wife for a career officer.

Maggie surveyed the fort with knowledgeable eyes. It was similar to others scattered across the frontier, a bastion of defense yet harshly out of place even in a rough environment. Frowning, she pondered that notion. Until then it had never occurred to her quite how bleak and unlovely a stockade and parade ground, along with its cluster of raw buildings, actually was.

The wind blew from the stables across the compound, directly toward the officers' quarters. A creek meandered through, a necessary adjunct at any time and particularly so in case of attack or siege. A few willows still fringed its banks, leaning to the prevailing wind. Whoever had designed the layout in the first place should have been equally observing when locating the living quarters, but had not been.

Indians could move across the land, hundreds at a time, with horses, dogs and tepees. They camped awhile, then went on, and the grounds were scarcely scarred, soon restored by sun and rain. Somehow white men rendered ugly not only their places of habitation but nearly everything with which they came in contact.

We could learn something from our red neighbors—if we only would, she reflected. Only we're too proud—and stupid.

With Mrs. Gallagher assisting, she erased the stains of travel, soaking in an inadequate tub, scrubbing briskly, preparing for supper. By rights her arrival should have been an occasion, in more ways than one. Visitors to remote outposts were rare and always welcome; doubly so when they wore skirts.

Normal procedure was for the wives of officers to arrange a ball, enjoying as gala a celebration as circumstances permitted. As a small girl she had snipped and pasted, helping build long chains of vari-colored paper to decorate a room, fashioning Japanese lanterns or artificial flowers, pulsing to the contagion of excitement. . . .

But here there were no wives. Lookout had been too far out, too perilous for women. Overton had assured her that, with changing conditions, reinforcements, such as he had just received would be commonplace. Once she became his wife, he hoped to change conditions permanently.

Even without a ball, the other officers would dine with them that evening, and she should be aflutter with expectancy at the anticipation in Overton's eyes, the certainty of the question he would press upon her at the first opportunity, hoping for a final answer—

Somehow it was all wrong, as barren as the parade ground. Whatever build-up there had been at the start of her journey had turned into a let-down, like a collapsing cake. Overton would be disappointed, and that was rather too bad. Although she had had the best of intentions, she decided that she had managed rather badly. But she had known since the evening before—actually since three days ago—what her answer must be.

Aware of a sudden flurry of excitement, she stepped to the door, looking out in the last of the sunlight. More visitors were arriving; these were clearly unexpected. Another ambulance had swung in at the gate and pulled to a halt, along with an escort of half a score of mounted men in blue. Uncomfortable as an ambulance was, it was the most luxurious conveyance usually available.

A lady was stepping down, alighting gracefully, which was something of a feat, even with a suggestion of majesty. Maggie Trout gasped.

Whatever she had expected, that her mother

should arrive there had been the farthest thing from her calculations. That she should unannounced, so swiftly upon her own heels, was still more surprising.

Mrs. Malcolm Trout was a good wife and mother, but at times a law unto herself. The colonel, philosophical by nature, had long since learned that, though he was the commandant of a post, there were bounds to his authority; in other words, that Melissa Trout had a mind of her own.

Startled, but gallant as befitted the occasion, Major Overton hastened to meet her, very much at a loss but doing his best.

Maggie, flying across the grounds, a sudden lump in her throat at sight of the lovely yet formidable lady who was her mother, was in time to overhear the exchange.

"Why, Mrs. Trout—dear lady, this is a most pleasant surprise, but a surprise nonetheless. We hadn't expected you—there was no word that you might be coming. I—"

"There was no time to send word, only to come," Melissa returned. "As soon as news of the Indians uprising reached us, I lost no time in setting out to remove my daughter as far as possible from such a dangerous location. I'm not blaming you, Major— at least not for failing to send word. I suppose there was no time."

She turned as Maggie came up, greeting her almost casually. "I was just behind you most of the way, though I covered in four days what you took six to cover. It was a relief to learn from your returning escort that you were being looked after by Lieutenant McChesney."

Overton's face, somewhat blank and bewildered up to then, darkened. There were those who, while considering Mrs. Trout a most estimable lady, deplored her occasional tactlessness.

"I understand your concern, my dear lady," Overton managed. "But actually there is nothing to apprehend in the way of danger—"

"After the slaughter of the innocents by men of your command, Major? A senseless massacre of women and children, grouped for protection under the American flag? And a provocation like that against so powerful a tribe as the Cheyennes?"

Clearly she was of a mind to say more and was restrained only by the demands of hospitality and army tradition, which she usually respected. Margaret regarded her mother with mingled affection, awe and a certain exasperation. On the whole, admiration and gratitude were uppermost. Melissa had voiced her own thoughts and opinions, though Maggie had felt no particular apprehension. Certainly she would not have slunk quickly away for the sake of her own welfare, even if an unlikely opportunity had presented itself.

But now that the chance was at hand, her mother having come for her with an escort, she certainly would not reject the deliverance. Here was one more proof of her parents' love, their very real concern at such a time. What really counted was that her position there, as a guest of Major Overton, had suddenly become difficult if not untenable.

It was Mrs. Trout's intention to set out promptly on the return the next morning, not back to the old fort which had been her husband's command and Maggie's home, but to a point more to the east and less distant, where they would rejoin the colonel, already on the first leg of his journey.

McChesney, as surprised as any, heard the news with mixed feelings. Despite her bluntness, he approved of what Melissa had said. It was no more than the truth, and he suspected that Colonel Trout harbored similar opinions. From what he had heard about him, Trout was no exponent of manifest destiny, and had it lain within his jurisdiction, he would have dealt promptly and strongly with so blatant an infraction of the rights of a friendly people.

McChesney had the opportunity for only a brief word with Maggie, and that came the next morning, as she and her mother and their escort prepared to set out. Major Overton, hovering in the background, was manifestly in a bad mood.

About to follow her mother and Mrs. Gallagher

into the ambulance, Maggie gave Mike her hand. Her words were breathless.

"Goodbye—Mike. The other evening—my mind was not quite made up. Now it is. I am *not* going to marry the major."

Her impulse was to add that he, like her, would probably be going East. Primly she resisted the temptation. That would not do for the colonel's daughter. Particularly for the colonel's daughter!

17.

Incredulous but elated at that hastily breathed admission, McChesney watched the departure of the women and their escort, striving to adjust to these developments. On one point there was no room for doubt. The colonel's lady was as impetuous and strong-willed as report had pictured.

As for Maggie—well, she was a credit to her ancestry. Maidenly modesty might have deterred her from speaking such words, but with the prospect of vast distances coming between them, and knowing how he felt, she had deemed it both fair and honorable to reveal something of her own mind. Like her mother, she was not bound by convention when the stakes were high enough.

His impulse was to follow hard on their heels, but that was not merely impractical but out of the question. The formalities of discharge must still be ob-

served before he would be free of the service, able to
dictate his own movements.

Some mail had awaited him, brought in along with
despatches during his absence. He had been too
busy and preoccupied to bother with it the evening
before. Now he opened a letter bearing the address
of the War Department. Its formidable appearance
was slightly tempered by the name neatly inscribed
at the corner, Lieutenant-Colonel Wisham Peters.

The name conjured up a flood of pleasant mem-
ories. Peters had been a fellow-officer, one of his
best friends. But of late they had lost touch with
each other.

The letter was in Peters' handwriting; in it he
explained his desk job, which was hardly to his liking, but which had certain compensations. Through
it he had been able to trace McChesney's whereabouts and was addressing him to request a favor.
Though it seemed unlikely that he could render it,
still he might keep his eyes and ears open.

Samuel Henry was a distant cousin of Peters;
moody and uncertain as a youth, he had become un-
predictable as he had grown older. He had taken off
for the West, sending back only an occasional letter
to his distracted family. Even those had ceased about
a year before, though their concern had not. Since
Sam Henry was a nephew to a United States Sena-
tor, and on the other side to Colonel Peters, a lot of

effort was being enlisted in an effort to trace him or discover his whereabouts.

He had last been reported as a guest at the ranch of Alexander McGillicuddy. If McChesney could institute inquiries and discover Henry's present whereabouts, Peters would be deeply grateful.

He enclosed what information he had which might prove helpful, adding in a postscript an additional item for possible identification. He always wore a silver bracelet on his left wrist. A part of the bracelet was in the shape of a bucking horse.

McChesney's brows drew together in sudden thought. He sat a while, in frowning concentration, and memory, hazy at first, cleared and focused. He had a notion that he had the answer to his friend's request, but one which Peters would find as distressing as the answer given Major Overton a short while before.

McChesney's mind had been upon other matters when he prowled the devastated battle ground near Two Buttes, following the discovery of his sister's body. He had needed to know how and why she had come to be there at such a time, and her involvement with others of the slain. He had rooted out the evidence and put it together. In the course of that investigation he had come upon the bodies of a number of the newly dead, giving them a brief but careful inspection.

One body, which he had taken to be Indian, had held his attention because of a bracelet on a wrist. That had seemed odd and out of place, and he had suspected that it might have been taken from a white victim. The oddity of its shape might well attract a warrior's fancy.

It had been stained and mud-encrusted, and he had not examined it very thoroughly, but it had certainly resembled a bucking horse, now that it was pointed out. Such a bracelet was too unusual to be a mere coincidence.

Other white men had joined the Indians, sometimes fighting with them. If Sam Henry had been counted odd, deliberately breaking off all communication with his own kin, that would explain it. He might well have been one of the victims at the Buttes.

Wisham Peters and the others would be interested in that information, but it was too serious a matter to send a report without checking more carefully. Which should not be too difficult. The McGillicuddys, Jim especially, might be able to help.

The request and his partial knowledge called for some changes of plan. Anger, as chill as the creeping ice along the fringes of a pond, had been congealing in him since that day when he'd stood before Orlando Overton with the body of his sister in his arms. That Overton had been genuinely shocked and contrite made no difference. Her death, and the wanton slaughter of others—now including Sam Henry—was Overton's responsibility. He had not given the order, but his attitude had condoned and encouraged such conduct on the part of his underlings.

McChesney's mind had been made up. Once out of uniform, he would tell Overton precisely what he thought of him—that he was a murderer, a bestial killer. Freed of the restraints of discipline, it would be a relief to deal man to man.

Now he was uncertain. Overton's trouble lay partly in his training, and as a soldier that perhaps was to his credit. Partly it stemmed from his state of mind; and however misguided, he was sincere. If these made it worse, still they needed to be considered.

And these last hours, Mike suspected, had been shattering for the major. He had been looking forward to an early marriage with Margaret Trout, and out of a clear sky, the colonel's lady had arrived to denounce him in almost as bitter terms as McChesney had intended to use, and to snatch away her daughter. At the least, Overton would be badly shaken.

That was an understatement. The experience had stunned him emotionally, upsetting his ego. He had paced the confines of his own quarters during the small hours of the night, raging one moment, uncertain the next. His impulse was to cross to where

Maggie and her mother were sleeping, to demand a clarification, an explanation. He must have an end to the sudden, dismaying uncertainty.

That course had been impossible; he had to wait until the morning. But the new day had found him brushed aside, the colonel's formidable lady taking charge, affording or allowing him no opportunity for a heart-to-heart talk, an understanding. At his protest that their departure at such a time was dangerous, he had met with disdain.

With grim desperation he had added a score of men to the escort commanded by Lieutenant Beasley. That was at once the best and the least that he could do. And his guests had departed with nothing quite understood or definite.

Haggard, tense from lack of sleep, he received McChesney with careful formality, proceeding with the necessary routine. He was almost at the end when a thought hit him; his mind was pierced by a sudden stab of jealousy.

He had sent this man to meet Margaret Trout and escort her to the fort. They had had three days together, time enough not merely to become friends, but for friendship to ripen into something more. And now, hard on the heels of Maggie's departure, Mc-Chesney also was ready to leave, obstensibly to head in the same direction—

On the surface, everything was logical and correct.

Maggie was going because her father was being trans-
fererd and her mother insisted. McChesney had
planned his move well in advance.

But after those few days together, Maggie was
throwing him over, breaking their engagement—

Actually, it had never been formalized, being at
best only a tentative understanding. The final ratifi-
cation for which Overton had looked had not come
about. Nor had she entirely refused him or broken
it off; merely left matters dangling, though by a more
tenuous thread than before.

He had intended to thank McChesney for serv-
ices rendered and to wish him well. That was a matter of courtesy. Instead he nodded curtly, returning
McChesney's final, ironical salute, suddenly hating
the man. . . .

The weather, which had been blustery and unpleasant during much of the expedition, had relented
once they were back at the fort, affording an almost
summer-like interlude for Margaret's journey. With
her departure, it was as though the elements re-
pented of so generous a mood. Winter swept out of
the north, snow pushed by gale-force winds. Temperatures dropped.

Overton shut himself up in his compound, along
with his men. He had a strong force now, and they
were reasonably well supplied. They could wait out

the moons of winter, much as the various tribesmen had planned to do, huddled in tepees, surviving on the fruits of the hunt.

For them the usual hardships would be multiplied. Much of the meat brought in by the hunters had been destroyed or left to rot, the skins which served in lieu of blankets burned or stolen. Many a hide, buffalo or deer, had shown behind saddles following the onset at the Buttes.

Overton had been careful to take no notice. Not only were the Indians being punished for having strayed from their reservations; in addition their agencies would use that as an excuse for furnishing fewer supplies, whatever the treaties might provide.

That many of the agents would pocket the difference was understood and accepted. It had become traditional, an accepted practice. Moreover, it taught a lesson, and if some starved or froze, in the long run it was the only possible solution to the problem.

Overton gave passing thought to those matters, shrugging aside the distasteful aspects. One good result was that the braves were too poor, too weak and hungry to prowl or raid. His methods had brought peace of a sort.

As a realist as well as a military man, he recognized it as more of a truce than peace. There had been rather wide-spread raiding in the wake of the affair at the Buttes. But now, blanketed under cold and snow, the land lay wide and empty, prowled only by four-footed predators. The stagecoaches had quit running, not alone because of the risks, but because in a denuded land there were no customers, no reason for continued service. Mail, which had been carried on a regular schedule, ceased to move.

Somewhat ponderously, the army functioned in its place. Convoys of supply wagons were slow but reasonably sure. Major Overton thumbed eagerly through his despatches when they came, only to turn in frustration and despair as he received no letter from Margaret. He had hoped that she would write, perhaps explain, affording him a chance to reply, perhaps to repair the damage.

Yet he recognized one vital fact. Maggie was like her father, who as an officer leaned to the philosophy of Mike McChesney rather than Overton's. Trout had no patience with manifest destiny, and scant liking for many of the methods applied in keeping order.

Overton took it for granted that Maggie had gone on with her folks. Then news reached him by a round-about report that she had not. She was still somewhere on the frontier, living with friends—and almost within reach. She had chosen to stay—

His first elation was tempered by the fact that she had not let him know. Belatedly, he had come to understand just how much she meant to him. It would have been good policy to pay more attention to her opinions, to follow a course which would have won her approval rather than condemnation.

Apparently it was too late. And he knew the reason. Mike McChesney.

Other reports indicated that McChesney was somewhere in the vicinity, not having gone East. Coupled with the news of Maggie Trout, to Overton that was only too revealing.

The weather had warmed, and snow was falling, a steady, blanketing storm. Through its haze, figures moved like ghosts across the parade ground. Noticing vague shapes, Overton questioned his orderly. The answer surprised him.

"Yes sir, someone did visit the post. Lieutenant McChesney."

"McChesney? You mean he's come and gone without even saying hello to his fellow-officers?"

"He was here hardly five minutes in all, sir. I understand that he brought a letter, asking that it be forwarded with the regular despatches when they go out. He requested that because there is no other mail service."

That was reasonable, particularly for a former officer. And considering the coldness of their parting, it was understandable that McChesney had not paid him a courtesy call.

Overton chewed at his underlip. Assailed by sudden suspicion, he swung about.

"Bring me the despatches—all of them. I want to check something."

He turned back from staring at the falling snow as the orderly returned. A glance at his empty hands turned him cold with apprehension.

"I'm sorry, sir. But our despatches were all ready to go, as it chanced, and they are on the way—Lieutenant McChesney's along with the others, of course."

18.

Obtaining the confirmation which he sought in regard to Samuel Henry proved more of a chore than McChesney had expected. Traveling alone was slow and difficult, hampered by bad weather, and finding Jim McGillicuddy had taken time. He had finally found him back at the ranch, but hardly in a cooperative mood.

"Why should I answer that question—supposin' that I was able to?" he countered. "By your own account, this Henry must have wanted to shed his name and start a new life. If he didn't want even his family to know, shouldn't his wishes be respected?"

"Generally I'd go along with you on that," McChesney granted. "On the other hand, they are concerned about him—and if, as I think, he is dead, it can make no difference to him now. So what is the harm in letting them know?"

"You may be right, and you, like him, have made it plain where you stand. I did meet him a couple of times. He had taken an Indian name and lived as one. I never asked his reasons or even his name. I'm not sure about it being Henry, but he was white, and he wore a bracelet with a bucking horse."

"I'll let them know. It seems to answer their question."

"One of those answers that's not very satisfying, eh? And now, with that out of the way, I suppose you'll be making a call upon a certain lady with no more waste of time, eh?" His eyes held a friendly twinkle.

"I don't know," McChesney admitted. "Probably I will go East. But from my old hometown to Washington is a long journey, and I have no sure reason to suppose that making it would be rewarding." Counting Jim a friend, he added frankly. "I have had no word of any sort."

"What better word could you ask than for her to stay on in this part of the country instead of going back with her folks?" Jim countered. "She had to have a mind of her own, and a reason. But if you don't sort of drift around one of these days, she may decide that you just aren't interested."

"Now what's this?" Mike was startled. "Are you telling me that she didn't go East? You can't mean—"

"I mean nothing, my friend, for life is too uncertain. But I have been told that she decided to stay on awhile with friends, and were I in your place I would seek a compelling reason."

Overton was suddenly frantic. For some time he had been in the grip of apathy and indecision, waiting in the hope that something might happen, waiting for some word to give hope or direction. Now, and perhaps too late, he had news, not at all of the sort he had looked for, but to his disordered imagination dangerous in the extreme.

"The gall of the man!" he muttered. "The insufferable nerve of him, to come back here, to make use of my despatch service to send out word that may destroy me!" His mind ranged frantically. McChesney had lingered on instead of leaving the country. For what possible reason other than to gather additional evidence with which to drag down the man whom he counted responsible for the murder of his sister—

Turning, he plunged out into the storm, to burst into the room where despatches were received, distributed and sent out. If what he supposed was correct, there was no time to lose.

Private Dix had handled such chores for the past year. A clerkly, almost timid man, he observed apprehensively the glare in the commandant's eyes and heard his wild questions as to why McChesney had been permitted to make unauthorized use of the despatch service. Shaken, for a time he could only stammer inarticulately. Overton controlled his own passion with an effort.

"I'm not blaming you," he said. "But this is im-

portant. Now think, man. This letter or despatch—
whatever it was that McChesney gave you—to whom
was it addressed?"

Dix resisted the impulse to swipe a sleeve across
a suddenly sweaty face.

"I remember that, sir. It was to a Lieutenant-
Colonel Peters—rather an unusual name, not William
or Wilbur—now I remember it, sir. Lieutenant-
Colonel Wisham Peters, in care of the War Department—"

"My God," Overton groaned, and made his way
blindly back to his own quarters. There he pondered
the significance of the disclosure, along with other
matters which he had recently learned. They seemed
to add up, inescapably, to one conclusion.

McChesney had disagreed with him, and strongly,
to the extent that he had chosen to quit the service,
casting aside his career. A man had to be strongly
motivated to take such drastic action. Even more
impelling, bad luck or a fatal chance had brought
McChesney's sister to the wrong place at the wrong
time, and since that moment McChesney had hated
him. . . .

Now he was striking back.

Lieutenant-Colonel Wisham Peters, of the War
Department, was a man of powerful connections,
occupying an influential position. After moving about
the country asking questions and digging up information, McChesney was reporting to him.

Undoubtedly he would detail the recent expedition and its fatal consequences, including the death of his sister. Charges would be preferred. The least that could be expected to follow would be an official inquiry, with the strong likelihood of a severe reprimand; the worst would be a court-martial and ruin. At best, his career would come to a halt, with further advancement or more favorable commands out of the question.

In the wrong hands, it would be easy to make out a case against him which could lead to dishonor and disgrace. Clearly McChesney was aiming at nothing less.

Hate was an impelling motive. Jealousy was equally potent. As he brooded by himself during weeks of inaction, the whole matter had become clear in Overton's mind. Too late, he had realized his mistake in sending McChesney to command the escort and bring Margaret Trout to the fort.

From that time, everything had changed. Now, of course, McChesney wanted her, and she was staying on, not too far away, instead of going with her parents; remaining, but not sending him even a word. It was only too obivous that she was waiting for McChesney to complete his gathering of evidence, then to join her—

Maybe he will, Overton gritted furiously. But before he does all these things, he'll find he has a fight on his hands. As for those despatches—

A solution had come to him. Already, his situation bordered on the desperate. Once those charges, along with proof, were in the hands of higher authority, nothing could stop the turning wheels. But if that letter failed to arrive—

That would give him time for counter-measures. And he'd take them now, losing no more time. Already he had loitered too long, but it might not be too late.

Bad as the weather was, there was little to apprehend from enemies, so a couple or three men, well-mounted, were usually sent with despatches. That had been the case in this instance, and they had been gone less than an hour.

Overton pondered, mentally grimacing. He didn't like this, but a desperate situation demanded desperate measures. He sent for Schmitt.

"McChesney's been snooping around ever since he left the service," he said. "His reasons are obvious—to cause trouble for you and me. He blames us for what happened to his sister—and now that he's sent those despatches to the War Department, it's rather obvious what they will contain."

Schmitt nodded his understanding. "I can catch up with the despatch riders," he said.

"Make sure that you do. You'll want only a few men—picked men. You'll have to move fast."

"Trust me to do that." Schmitt wheeled, then turned back and saluted. "I'm on my way, sir."

Like Overton, he knew what had to be done. Once an inquiry was set in motion, it would lead almost inevitably to a court-martial, for both of them. This was not a time for scruples.

The wind was out of the east, an icy breath full in their faces. They bowed their heads and held their horses to a ground-devouring pace, and Schmitt, ignoring the frost which thickened from his breath while icicles hung to his mustache, pondered how best to execute his assignment. Once the despatch riders were overtaken, he could take over, but from the start he had known that he would follow no such simple procedure.

Among the despatches would be letters, including McChesney's, so that technically at least the riders carried the United States mail. Once a despatch sack was sealed and entrusted to a messenger, only the properly constituted authorities had any right to tamper with it.

It was unlikely, but if he took those despatches from them, one or more of the trio, at some future time, might talk. It was only prudent to anticipate difficulties and guard against them.

He had picked the trio who carried the despatches, choosing them for their knowledge of the country, their stamina and endurance under severe conditions.

Private Gray Horse was a full-blooded Indian;

Schmitt was of the opinion that he might be a Crow, though he was not sure, nor did it matter. An Indian was an Indian.

Private LaBrie was a half-breed. As for the corporal in charge, he might or might not be white. Since the three were friends who worked well together, who was to say that he was not a 'breed as well?

It did not occur to Schmitt that, in pursuing the despatch riders, he and his men might also be followed. That notion had come to Overton almost before they were out of sight. By going himself, he'd make sure there were no slip-ups.

Each trail showed plainly in the snow. First there were three horses, held mostly at a trot where the going was good. In places where the snow was deeper, they had gone single file. Six more double pairs of hoofs made a more beaten path. For Overton, keeping carefully back out of sight but pressing hard, the trail was easy.

The winter dark was beginning to close, thickened by freshly falling snow, as the pursuit paid off. Schmitt nodded to himself in silent approval. It could not have been better.

Squinting sharply through the gloom, one of his men started to speak, then, seeing Schmitt's face, closed his lips. The captain's mood was not conducive to unnecessary comments, and it probably did not matter that the sign showed five or six horses running ahead, instead of three. No plainsman, Schmitt was taking no notice.

Willows made a break in the flat field of white, lifting in a darker sweep. The creek they marked was lost under ice and snow. Schmitt swung, leading the way to the far side of the stream, across from where the despatch riders rode. They were pulling up, obviously intending to make use of a fuel supply to boil coffee and warm themselves, perhaps even to camp for the night. The figures looked ghost-like.

Schmitt moved his own men into position; then his voice rang out harshly with the order. A pony whinnied in high fright as the rifles blasted. The tiny fire which had targeted the victims flickered and was gone.

19.

Questing about the country for news of Sam Henry had been a tedious job, but McChesney had not begrudged the effort. Colonel Peters was his friend, and this was a chance to return past favors.

The stop at the fort to leave his letter for forwarding had brought an unexpected dividend. There had been a letter for him, and the name, in a fine clear handwriting at the upper corner, had caused his pulse to quicken.

Having read and re-read the missive, he lost no time in setting out, heading in the same general direction as would presently be taken by the despatch riders. It occurred to him that it might be pleasanter as well as prudent to wait and travel along with them, but he was driven by a sudden yeasty impatience. It seemed to him that too much time had been wasted already.

Overton was a man driven, like his own savagely spurred horse. Ignoring the barely veiled wonder of those who carried out his orders, he gave no instructions, offered no explanation. They might think what they chose and be damned What he was about was nobody's business but his own.

It was a simple matter to follow the well-beaten trail in the snow, alternately spurring, then allowing his horse a breather, never quite long enough for the exertions he demanded of it. The falling snow rendered him all but invisible, shutting away any view of those ahead. Neither Schmitt nor his men would be able to look back and guess that they were spied upon.

Reason assured him that such a ride was foolish, but he had to know what happened, to make sure that there was no further bungling. Too much hinged on the events which would take place during the hours immediately ahead. If anything should go wrong, he would be ruined.

It did no good to remind himself that Schmitt was dependable, a cold-blooded machine, with fully as much at stake as himself. He had to know.

Once he was sure that the threat had been removed, he could pursue new plans. He would seek out Margaret Trout. To his increasing surprise and wonder, she had been increasingly and persistently in his mind.

He would find a way to reassure her; to convince her, where he had almost succeeded before. He must win her.

How he did not know; only that it had to be done. Once he'd determined to win her because her father was of high rank and influential, and such a relationship could help his own career. That she was a personable lady and accustomed to army life, the perfect helpmate for a career officer, had been merely a pleasant dividend.

Now all of that had become secondary. It was the woman herself who counted. She had somehow become vital to his hopes and aspirations, to his emotional and physical needs.

She had remained in the country instead of going East; he hoped desperately that it was a good omen. The only other reason for her staying on would be McChesney—

Curse the man! Overton recognized another change in himself, which had come about gradually, almost unnoticed, but was nevertheless grimly real. He hated McChesney, and if he got in the way, then he'd have to suffer the consequences. Nothing was going to stop him.

Darkness was closing as he rode, but his horse instinctively followed the beaten trail. It started, head jerking, as guns volleyed raggedly in the night. The belches of crimson from their muzzles were not so distant but that they showed, tiny licking tongues.

More shots followed in an uneven tempo. Schmitt was doing his job, as he could always be depended on to do it, without scruple. Again he had been given no precise orders, and again none had been needed.

Those additional shots, a mopping-up of stragglers, were proper. It was only prudent to make certain that no stragglers remained, no possible witnesses who might later set a hang-noose about a neck.

Overton remembered then to call out warningly, explaining his approach. In the gloom it would be easy to mistake him for another straggler.

Schmitt exclaimed sharply, his voice ragged with surprise and annoyance. An instant later he had himself under control.

"It's lucky you called, Major," he said. "I didn't know who might be coming—and I don't like to take chances. For some reason or other, those fools tried to fire on us, and we had no choice but to shoot back. I'm not even sure who they were—"

Such an explanation was a justification for his actions and would be hard to disprove. Schmitt had chosen carefully before setting out, picking men who were not only trustworthy but personally loyal to himself. Now they would be bound by an added need for silence. To admit the possibility of anything other than a mistake, after wiping out the despatch riders, would be suicidal.

"Mistakes can occur in such weather," Overton concurred shortly. He did not bother to explain why he had followed. He was the commandant. Now that he was there, he'd make doubly sure of the success of the mission, taking charge of the despatches.

One of Schmitt's men had dismounted, bending above one of the darker figures outstretched, almost hidden in the snow. He cried out, a short, dog-like yelp of surprise, as though he had been kicked unexpectedly. Even in the gloom his face appeared ashen as he straightened.

"What's the matter?" Schmitt demanded angrily. The sheer consternation in that cry had shaken him.

"A—theres' been a mistake," was the stammered reply. "Look, sir. I don't know where he came from— how he could have been here—"

Schmitt dismounted and looked in turn and was equally shaken.

"It's McChesney," he said. "Lieutenant McChesney."

Overton, believing yet refusing to trust their testimony, looked too. Shocked, he could guess at the explanation. After his visit to the fort, McChesney must have headed east, finally stopping to build a fire, to cook a meal. The others had overtaken him—

"How is he?" Overton dared not look closer.

"Dead, sir. But no one guessed—"

Triumph welled in Overton, replacing the initial dismay. In a sense, it was too bad; regrettable, in fact. He suffered a twinge at the realization that these weeks had worked a change in him. From the start, he had been reconciled to the killing of Indians as a necessary means to an end. But removing white men, even under the prod of necessity, was not quite the same.

Once he would have recoiled in horror. Now he could mentally shrug. A soldier's business was to kill, under the spur of necessity.

Actually, this was turning into a piece of incredible luck. All along, McChesney had been the stumbling-block, the one obstacle in his way. Now he would have a clear path—

He turned away, shaking his head. Death was no respecter of persons.

Stumbling as his foot encountered a yielding object, all but buried in the snow, Overton recovered, then bent lower. At that instant the remnants of the fire flared, and the spreading light revealed another face. Overton's cry rang harsh and high, as had the private's moments before. Shaken, wrenched by tearing sobs, he dropped to his knees, knowing already, as he had been reminding himself, that death was final.

How it might have happened that she too had been there he did not understand, and it no longer really mattered. Somehow they must have communicated, have been journeying to meet each other.

The face of Margaret Trout looked curiously relaxed and peaceful in the brief flare of the light.